Murder at North Pond

Copyright © 2022 by London Lovett

All rights reserved.

No part of this book may be reproduced in any form or by any electronic or mechanical means, including information storage and retrieval systems, without written permission from the author, except for the use of brief quotations in a book review.

ISBN: 9798412628202

Imprint: Independently published

Frostfall Island Map by Hanna Sandvig

MURDER AT NORTH POND

FROSTFALL ISLAND
COZY MYSTERY SERIES

LONDON LOVETT

Now and then we had a hope that if we lived and were good, God would permit us to be pirates.

Mark Twain

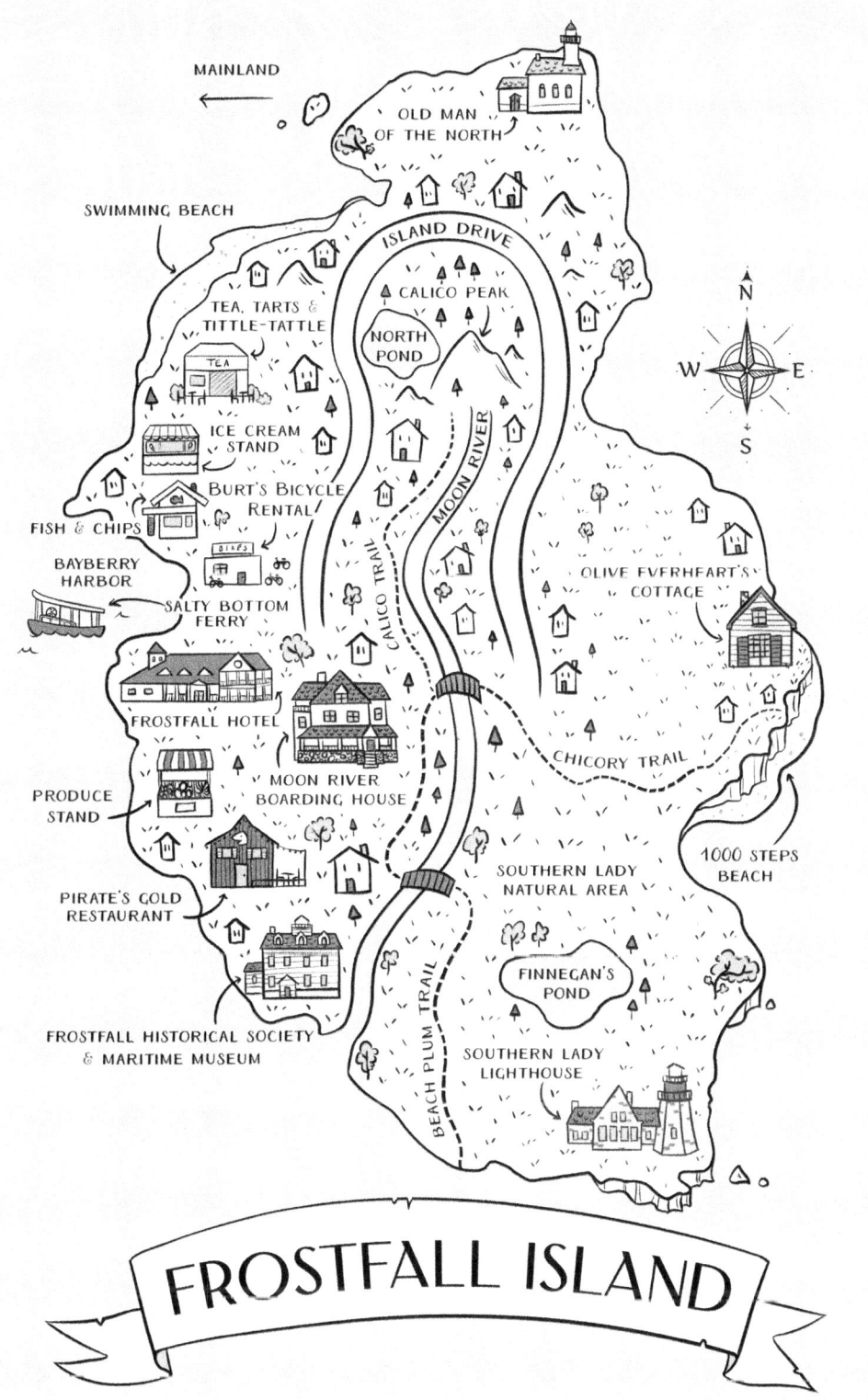

one

THE SUN WINKED at me from the horizon just moments before obliterating the peach colored streaks of dawn and erasing the perfect shadowy lighting from my work in progress. The sweet pepperbush would have to wait until tomorrow. Its deep green, toothy leaves seemed to relax as I packed up my watercolors as if it knew it had been sitting for a portrait. It was weeks too early for the plant's crowning glory, a tall, white spike of flowers, but I preferred to catch nature just before it went from inconspicuous to glorious. It was like spotting and admiring a movie star long before anyone else noticed their potential.

I snapped shut the tray of watercolors and tucked my paper pad under my arm. "Well, Huck, guess it's time to head back." The dog tilted his head side to side trying to decide whether the all important word 'cookie' had come up in my last few words. Deciding I hadn't mentioned one, he trotted on ahead of me, his bobbed tail pirouetting behind him as if he sported a long, fluffy tail.

Huck was such an odd mix of breeds. His rough, mottled coat and amber eyes gave him the look of a feral dog, one that belonged somewhere in the Australian Outback or African Serengeti rather than on an island. Michael and I laughed when we spotted the dog at the rescue. It was love at first sight… for me at least. Michael took some convincing. But Huck, already two at the time and on his third home, knew how to warm his way into Michael's heart, greeting him joyfully after a long day on the water, resting his head in his lap whenever Michael was feeling down and even, on occasion, bringing him one of his special doggie treats. Michael would pretend to eat it so as not to disappoint Huck. The dog understood that he had to do things right this time, another family, another month at the shelter waiting for someone to fall for him and take him home was out of the question. He needn't have worried though. For me, the attachment was so instant, so profound, I knew Huck had finally found his forever home.

Huck pounced into some shrubs and scared a pair of robins from their shelter. Robins, with their marmalade colored bellies, were always the first to arrive. Spring was just starting to peel back the dreary layers of winter. It wouldn't be long before Frostfall Island burst to life with all the critters lucky enough to call it home.

Frostfall Island was one of those elusive places no one could find on a map. It was neither north nor south, east nor west. It wasn't too close to the equator and was still far enough from the North Pole. Frostfall wasn't lush and humid like a tropical island. At the same time, it wasn't a mass of frozen tundra like Iceland. The island's mood was fickle, depending on the weather and where you stood. If you peered across the moors on the northeast corner during a frosty fog, you could half expect a dark and brooding Heathcliff to wander out of the gothic mist. But on the sunny, westernmost edge of the island, a bike ride and a double scoop of mocha fudge marble seemed more in order. Most people, even on the Atlantic coast, had never heard of Frostfall Island, and we liked it that way. Michael used to say Frostfall was like that small Hawaiian island that no one could remember the name of but that was far more beautiful than its popular sisters, Oahu and Maui. There were numerous islands off the eastern coast, some that were too rocky and wild to inhabit and some with real estate in such high demand only the wealthy could afford it. Frostfall was somewhere in between. It had its own little place in the Atlantic universe, and once I'd landed here, I knew I, too, had found my forever home.

Huck trotted ahead but stopped at the curve halfway along the trail. He knew I would stop there too, the same spot I paused at every time we hiked along Beach Plum Trail. My breath produced cloudy puffs in the early morning chill. The tin tray of watercolors had grown cold in my hand by the time I reached Huck.

The dog was staring off at the horizon, as if he was remembering that fateful day, the day that Huck and I stood to wave at Michael as his fishing trawler rounded the southern tip of the island. His glossy, yellow rain slicker glistened in the cloud-filtered sunlight as he waved to us from his wheelhouse. Huck and I stood on that same curve everyday for a year, no matter how thick and cold the fog or how brittle and sharp the wind. I'd blow Michael good luck kisses, and Huck would bark his goodbyes. Gosh, how Michael hated the sound of Huck's bark. "That dog's bark sounds like someone chewing on a mouthful of gravel," he would complain with a laugh. Michael's laugh was the thing I missed the most about him, along with a million other things like the way he buttered toast and poured coffee for me every morning and brought it to me in bed so my feet didn't have to hit the cold floor before I'd warmed myself with breakfast. Like the way he'd hold me as we stood out on the front porch listening to the springtime frogs or the fall crickets. Or the way he'd bring me something special, a trinket, a shell or a pretty tea cup from the mainland after he'd docked to weigh his catch.

That day, the day Huck and I watched Michael float off for the last time, there was something not quite right about my husband's smile. Even his wave seemed less exuberant. He never reached up to scoop my wind-borne kiss from the salty air.

I'd gone over the details of those last few moments so often it had drained me. The sun had tried badly to break past the gray clouds streaking the sky. The sea was a deep, emerald green, and it was choppy enough to make the *Wild Rose*, the twenty-foot trawler and Michael's pride and joy, waddle from side to side like a fat duck. Three great black-backed seagulls hovered low next to the boat, determined to *help* with the catch. For months, whenever I spotted a gull, I interrogated the bird (and the bird would look at me, rightfully, as if I was crazy) to see if it had been one of those three gulls. It seemed they would be the only souls on earth, the only witnesses that might be able to tell me what happened that fateful day when Michael sailed off and never returned.

A wind pushed a strand of my auburn hair across my cheek. I flicked it back and gazed out one last time, past the edge of the rocky bluffs, over the black iron cap of the Southern Lady Lighthouse and along the rippling blue water. I wasn't sure why I always stopped to look. Maybe I was just trying to get back that feeling, that joy I felt knowing that after a long, hard day Michael would climb the porch steps, curse a little as he pulled off his tight work boots and lumber into the house smelling like salt and diesel and love.

I patted Huck's head. He pushed against my hand, hoping for a scratch behind his ear. I obliged him for a moment. "We need to get back, buddy. I've got to start breakfast."

Beach Plum Trail, my favorite on the island, gently glided up the center of the island. It was dotted with the Kelly green leaves of beach plums, the cheery little fruit-bearing plants it was named for. Delicate white blossoms were already making their debut, whispering promises of crimson and purple plums, a fruit that was most assuredly a matter of taste. I found them bitter but others found them sweet.

If you walked south on Beach Plum Trail, you would end up at the southern lighthouse, one of two on the island. North would take you to Moon River and the bridge leading to Calico Trail. And Calico Trail led home, my home. Michael had inherited the Moon River Boarding House from his grandparents. The three-story Victorian boasted fifteen rooms, eight fireplaces and enough creaks and rattles to scare off even the most stalwart of ghosts. Admittedly, after my slick, modern apartment in the city, the house, with its drafty windows, moaning pipes and the occasional unexplained noise, took some getting used to. I'd given up more than my city life when I followed Michael to Frostfall Island. I'd given up a successful career in finance, a boring, high stress career that I was just as happy to leave.

Michael's fishing business was so dependent on the will of the ocean, I thought we needed to supplement our income. His grandmother had run a successful boarding house. While I'd never imagined myself running a boarding house while flitting between economics and business management classes, the idea soon grew on me. Michael had ruled against it, vehemently, insisting we could manage on whatever his catch brought in. I'd given up on the idea until Michael disappeared. Then, I found myself alone with a large, empty house in constant need of repair.

I started the boarding house a year after Michael was lost at sea. My tenants, a collection of mismatched, eccentric and the most wonderful people I'd ever met, were now my family. One of them, literally. My older sister, Cora, had joined us after the death of her second husband. The first hubby had died too. In her defense, they were both incredibly old... and incredibly rich. They'd also both had previous families, ex-wives, children and grandchildren who made sure that my sister didn't leave their posh estates with more than she could carry.

    Cora Cromwell, a name she kept from the second husband because of its prominence in Great Britain's history, was the candy coated crowned jewel of the family. Growing up, it had just been the two of us, trudging back and forth across town to stay at Mom's during the week and Dad's for the weekend. My mom was sure my sister's beauty would lead her to Hollywood or a lucrative modeling career. Instead, Cora took the much simpler route to a wealthy lifestyle. She was much better at saying 'I do' than 'I can'. Her second wedding cost more than eight hundred thousand dollars, including her fifty thousand dollar designer dress dotted with diamonds (she had to return the dress to the estate upon her husband's death). It was such an elaborate affair, she'd had no choice except to sign the draconian prenuptial agreement her future step-children forced upon her just seconds before the start of the ceremony. After all, no bride runs off when there are swans with gold tails and white horses dressed as unicorns waiting for you at the reception. It was the fairy tale wedding she'd always dreamed of, only instead of Prince Charming standing in his velvet lined cape and gold crown at the blossom covered altar, ninety-one-year-old Walter Cromwell waited, hunched and supported by both his sons (who were also old enough to be the bride's father). Still, my sister walked out with her radiant smile and obscenely expensive dress and sparkled like the diamonds on her gown. There was a collective gasp as the guests caught sight of the gorgeous bride. My dad kept pulling at his tight collar and shaking his head at the ridiculous spectacle. Mom wept with joy at the sight of her beautiful daughter. At least, I thought it was joy. It might have had to do with the prenuptial that would leave Cora destitute upon the death of her husband, an event that appeared to be not too far in the distant future.

My sister had fared better with her first marriage, managing to leave the funeral with a two million dollar check. Cora was never one to be called thrifty or cheap. She quickly spent the money on designer clothes, cars, jewelry and luxury vacations. My mom never had quite the same amount of praise for me as she had for Cora. It was true the only thing we shared were our green eyes. I was my parents' reliable, practical daughter. My mom's most glowing description of me to date was—"Anna, my sweet, you're tall but not too tall, thin but not too thin and plain but not too plain." One day, while we were out looking for dresses for Cora's first wedding, she came up with a real zinger—"Anna, if you turn your head just right and the sun shines just so, you're actually quite pretty." I'd laughed at the time telling her that it seemed all the stars in the universe had to line up for me to be passably pretty. She had the nerve to be hurt that I wasn't overjoyed at her compliment.

Huck led the way at a full trot. The new morning sun glinted off Finnegan's Pond, a small natural pond just off the trail and bordering a vast open space teeming with plants and wildlife. Ahead of me, toe nails clicking on the wooden bridge over Moon River alerted me to the fact that my dog was in need of a nail trimming. Naturally, I wouldn't tell him that or even dare to spell out the words nail trimming until it was time for the deed. The last time I'd pulled out the clippers and clicked them in my hand to loosen them up, Huck ran out his door and into the trees behind the house. He stayed there until all threats of a pedicure had disappeared.

I stopped halfway over the bridge and gazed down at the crystal clear water dashing and dancing over the rocks below. A pair of mallards floated along, happy to have the river free of snow and ice for a change.

As much as I preferred to stay out in nature on a sunny spring morning, I'd procrastinated long enough. My band of merry misfits would be gathering at the kitchen table soon, and something told me, on this particular morning, they might just have a surprise planned.

two

I PAUSED to admire the Moon River Boarding House in all its vintage, charismatic glory. Even with the collection of sad memories; the evening I sat in front of a dying fire waiting for Michael to return, wondering what on earth was taking so long for him to come home to me and waiting urgently to hear him drop his heavy, wet boots on the porch; me standing hopefully, anxiously on the porch as the young coast guard walked up the path, wet, cold and nervous about delivering dreadful news that the *Wild Rose* had been found stuck on rocks thirty miles east of Frostfall, no skipper onboard; the wake we held after seven years had passed and Michael was officially declared dead, people drifting silently, sadly in and out of the mahogany front door carrying casseroles, pound cakes and condolences. Even with those memories clinging to the ivory white edges of the house, I was always happy to see it.

For a long while, the Victorian beauty and Huck were my

only family, the only two souls on earth who felt and understood my sorrow. And yes, the house had a soul. I was sure of it. She knew exactly when to comfort me, when to wrap her big Victorian arms around me and keep me warm and safe. At the same time, she knew exactly when to push me out the door into the revitalizing sunshine or a brisk, energetic breeze.

The house was surrounded by a massive porch, held in place with shiny white columns and a weather safe overhang. It was an assortment of steeply pitched roofs and a patchwork of double-hung windows. For a stately old Victorian, she lacked some of the whimsical gingerbread embellishments, the standard adornments of other ladies from her time. I preferred the simpler, more austere look to the over accessorized Victorian.

Huck bounded up the steps ahead of me and scratched at the screen door. Something he'd been told a million times not to do but he'd dismissed every time as silly. A long, silver garland dotted with equally silver balloons greeted me at the entrance to the kitchen. I spotted the words *Congratulations on your Silver Wedding Anniversary* written in fancy white script across the metallic balloons. I stepped into the heart of the house, a massive eat-in kitchen.

Opal's fiery red hair spiked up from her head as she leaned over a plate of chocolate covered strawberries. (There was more chocolate on the plate… and my kitchen counters than the fruit.) Huck shot past me alerting Opal to my arrival. Her face popped up. She hadn't, as she liked to say, put on her face yet, a heavy layer of makeup that bordered on theatrical. Her eyes rounded behind her purple rimmed glasses. "Oh, Winston, the birthday girl is here. Surprise," she said, somewhat past the point of actual surprise.

Winston spun around from the sink, a wash rag in his hand and a baby pouch hanging in front of his chest. The two baby robins he'd been feeding around the clock poked their patchy bald heads above the edge of the pouch to see what all the excitement was about. Winston's big brown eyes smiled above his white, toothy grin. At thirty, Winston still retained that wonderful glow of youth, the youth I was apparently leaving behind to head into the next decade of my life, the one where you really started to feel that downhill pull. I had dreaded turning thirty. Now I would have given anything to be turning thirty instead of forty.

"Happy birthday, Anna," Winston cheered. He waved his arm toward the strawberries. "We made your favorite, and don't worry, I'll get this cleaned up in a jiffy." One thing about working with melted chocolate, it always somehow managed to get everywhere, as evidenced by the large streak on Winston's forearm, only to be outdone by the streak across his forehead. At least his thick blond hair appeared to have avoided the chocolate. He smiled down at his two baby birds. "William, Kate, did you say happy birthday?"

Opal scoffed. "Did you seriously name those birds after the Duke and Duchess of Cambridge?"

Winston's brow creased. "Who?"

I winked at Opal. "I think it's just a coincidence."

"Have a seat." Winston pulled out my usual chair at the table. "I've made coffee."

I walked across the room to the desk in the corner of the kitchen. It was cluttered with the week's menus, grocery lists and utility bills. I scooted the mess aside and put down my paint and artwork. Winston poured me a cup of coffee and set the cream next to it.

Opal's smile lines deepened on her face. "How are you feeling? I remember my fortieth like it was yesterday. The staff at the middle school I taught at left a cane and one of those old-fashioned hearing horns on my desk. They also brought my favorite chocolate torte. Delicious cake. I think that's why I remember the day so well."

"I'm not quite ready for the cane or hearing horn, but I did notice another few strands of silver this morning in the mirror."

Opal tilted her head and gave me a sympathetic smile. "It's cute that you call them silver instead of—you know—the color that should not be named."

"Yep, I'm sticking with silver."

Winston and his tiny friends joined us. William and Kate slipped back into the warmth of the baby pouch. Winston worked at the Frostfall Wildlife Rescue, a non-profit that took in all manner of creatures. Very often, when a baby animal needed extra or round the clock attention, Winston brought the animal home. None of us minded. In fact, we looked forward to the parade of baby squirrels, harbor seals and even, on occasion, young deer.

"Speaking of silver." Winston glanced up at the silver balloons hanging above his head with a good degree of consternation. "The plan was to decorate with purple and pink balloons, two of your favorite colors." He turned his dismayed expression to his party partner. "Opal was in charge of decorations, and I was in charge of strawberries."

"You took the easier job," Opal said with a haughty chin lift. "There were no purple or pink balloons anywhere on the island." Opal looked at me apologetically. "Becky Grubbs had some decorations left from their silver anniversary party. Can you believe she's been married to that dull man for a quarter of a century? I'd rather be married to a pile of bricks."

Opal had been married once, to a teacher she worked with. None of us knew much about him except that his name was John and after ten years of marriage he realized he was more in love with Gregory Everett, the football coach, than his wife. The divorce was quick and, from all accounts, amiable.

"I thought once, for this special occasion, you might leave your room and your marathon of movie classics to head to the mainland. There's a party shop just two blocks from the ferry stop," Winston continued.

Opal shivered visibly at the thought of a ferry ride. "You know that ferry ride makes me seasick."

I reached for a strawberry. The chocolate was still sticky. "Everything is perfect." I took a bite of the treat and winked at both of them. "So good and I love the silver decorations. They match the strands in my hair."

Opal grinned with satisfaction and lifted a wafer thin package off her lap. It was wrapped with one of her silk scarves. Opal tended to dress as if she'd just walked off the set of a silent movie. And, in her mind, she had. About ten years ago, a vivid dream convinced Opal Barlow that she had once walked the earth as Rudolph Valentino, the early century movie star known for his good looks and Italian charm. He died young and tragically. Opal decided, quite confidently, that she had been Valentino in a previous life. None of us argued the point. After all, we certainly didn't have evidence to disprove it.

Opal beamed as she handed me her gift. "I'll need the scarf back," she noted.

I smiled and untied the scarf, the pink silk slipped away from a glossy photo of Rudolph Valentino. It was signed *Happy Birthday, Anna, love Rudy* in Opal's distinctly feminine handwriting. It was my third 'autographed' photo of the movie star. The autographed photos had become a slight problem when Opal suddenly decided she could sell glossy, autographed photos of the star as if they were authentic. She argued with us for a bit, insisting that they were technically authentic, but when the possibility of forgery and felony was brought up, she ended her business. Now, the rest of us were on the receiving end of the five dozen glossy photos she had ordered in anticipation of high demand for a Valentino autograph.

The upstairs pipe creaked as the shower went on in the women's bathroom. We had two in the house. The Victorians were bigger on sitting rooms and parlors than on showering. We'd designated one bathroom with shower and claw foot tub for the women of the house and one, more modernized, for the men. The whole setup worked well.

"That will be my sister getting up for breakfast." I finished the cup of coffee. "Thank you both so much for the lovely treat. I've got to get breakfast started. Eggs and hash browns sound all right?" I stood up and carried my cup to the sink. My white porcelain farm sink was more chocolate than porcelain.

"I feel bad," Winston said. "We should be making you breakfast."

I gazed down at the mess. "Oh no, you've already done enough, Winston. I love my strawberries and my silver balloons."

I sighed to myself. Forty, when did that happen?

three

THE BUTTERY SCENT of eggs and hash browns mingled with the metallic smell of the balloons and the rich scent of chocolate. The back door opened and Tobias walked inside. His thin hair stood up from his mostly bald scalp. The early morning sun had turned it pink, along with his nose.

"Toby, you're going to need to start wearing a hat again when you go for your morning swim," I noted.

Tobias reached up and patted his head. "You're right. I'll put that on my reminder board." Tobias was short and slight, and though he was fifty, he had the physique of a twelve-year-old boy. He kept trim and young with long morning swims at the beach. Aside from when he had the sniffles or a headache and as long as the weather permitted, he went everyday without fail. He insisted it cleared his head for working with numbers. Tobias was an accountant and the town treasurer, two jobs he took quite seriously. And rightfully so.

"I'll just get showered and changed. Breakfast smells good." Tobias hadn't noticed the silver balloons until he walked under them. "Oh right, happy birthday, Anna." He bowed his head formally. Tobias, or Toby as we called him, tended to be awkward in most social situations. However, when it was just the two of us, that social anxiety disappeared, and he could be quite informative and a good conversationalist as long as he wasn't talking about numbers.

"Thank you. Breakfast is almost done. If you see my sister floating around in all her lavish finery tell her soft boiled eggs are ready." Cora never liked her eggs scrambled. She said scrambled eggs were too chaotic. An interesting choice of word, considering the last ten years of my sister's life.

Tobias nodded again, awkwardly, as if we were mere strangers, then headed to the stairs.

The click-clack of Cora's heels tapped the steps as she descended them. She flounced into the kitchen sparkling like bubbly cream soda in her camel colored sequin dress with a high collar and sleek pencil bodice. A thin gold belt finished the look. This was one of her more common day dresses, like my blue cotton shift with the small coffee stain on the hem and the sewn tear on the bodice. Only Cora's casual day dress was more suited to a Hollywood premiere, while mine was suited for a cup of coffee with a friend. I always called this particular selection from her closet her Ginger dress because it reminded me of the one Ginger, the movie star, wore on Gilligan's island.

Cora's wardrobe, a collection of designer dresses all too formal for everyday wear, were the only remnants of her short-lived stints as the wife of billionaires. I'd finally convinced her to put most of her fine jewelry in a safety deposit box. Not that I worried about anything happening to it at Moon River, but it seemed entirely too careless to leave a fortune in platinum, gold and diamonds just lying around the house. She had kept her diamond and platinum watch out of the box. It glittered on her thin wrist as she pushed a long blonde curl back behind her ear and stared up at the balloons. Her emerald green gaze looked wryly my direction.

"Now, I know you're not twenty-five because that would make me twenty-seven." She laughed airily, something she'd learned to do at all the social luncheons she had to sit through as a trophy wife.

I laughed, too, only mine was far more organic. "If I was twenty-five, I wouldn't be standing here with a spatula in my hand and an apron around my waist, and you wouldn't be twenty-seven, you'd be thirty-one, my dear older sister. You keep erasing years. Pretty soon, I'll be the older sister."

"I can't possibly be that old. Mirrors don't lie."

"Tell that to the Queen in Snow White," Opal quipped. Opal was an old movie expert. She spent the larger part of her day watching classic films.

Cora's dress shimmied, and the sequins caught all the different sources of light in the kitchen. She pulled out her chair to sit at our long pine table. I'd purchased the table, one that could fit ten people, at an antique auction on the mainland. I had to pay Frannie, the captain of the ferry, for six seats on the *SS Salty Bottom* just to get it across the channel. It was worth every penny. It had all the fabulous scars and marks and patina from a lifetime of being a dining room table. Sometimes, when I was alone in the kitchen, I could almost imagine all the conversations people had had at the table floating above it in those funny cartoon bubbles.

I carried a soft boiled egg and plate of hash browns to my sister. She smiled up at me with that picture perfect smile, the one that had all the boys in the neighborhood riding their bikes in circles in front of the house. "Happy birthday, sis. Love you." She blew me a kiss.

I blew one back. We'd always had our differences, but we were as close as two sisters could be. I was thrilled when Cora decided to move into Moon River.

Cora tapped her egg with a spoon to remove the crown. "When is the new boarder arriving?"

"Sometime today." I scooped eggs onto a plate and handed them to Winston first because he needed to get to work. Opal, on the other hand, tended to linger at the breakfast table all morning, occasionally filling my head with stories of her life, both lives, actually. I now knew far more about Charlie Chaplin and Lillian Gish than I ever hoped to know. And Opal always spoke with great confidence and clarity about her past life friends, so I never questioned any of it.

"I don't mind saying, I'm a little concerned about this new addition," Opal said. "He'll be a complete stranger."

I handed Opal her plate. "You mean like you were the first time you walked into the boarding house two years ago?"

"Yes, but that's different. I'm me. And this is a man. You know they're never as congenial and easy to get along with." Opal turned the lazy Susan in the middle of the table so that the butter and marmalade were in front of her. While most people opted for ketchup or hot sauce on their eggs, Opal preferred a sweeter version. She plopped a big spoon of tangy orange marmalade on her eggs and topped off her hash browns with a large scoop of butter.

"And this is where *this* man bows out of the conversation. We've got a baby harbor seal and its mother coming in this morning. They were caught in the reef below the lighthouse and got pretty bruised up." Winston carried his plate to the sink. "I'll see you all for dinner."

"Have a good day, Winston, and thanks again for the delicious strawberries," I called after him through the back screen door.

Cora got up to refresh her coffee. "I, for one, am pleased that the new boarder is male."

Opal and I exchanged knowing glances. Neither of us was terribly surprised about the position she had taken.

"You do realize that he won't be a billionaire," I said. "Not even a millionaire. Although, he did pay six months in advance. I told him it wasn't necessary since his room was month to month. After all, what if he doesn't like the place, I said to him in my email. We've only spoken through email. He wrote back that as long as he had a bed, a place to shower and some good meals he was happy. That is how I know he's not a successful businessman. I've known a few in my day, and they are the most spoiled, persnickety bunch of men in the world."

Tobias had deciphered that our conversation was about men, so he cleared his throat loudly as he entered the kitchen. I picked up the plate I'd prepared especially for him with the eggs on one side, piled neatly so that none of the fluffy yellow stuff touched the crispy, golden hash browns. Tobias could not eat any foods that had touched another food. It was something I'd learned rather quickly when I handed him his first plate, a plate with spaghetti and meatballs. He looked at the tomato-y mishmash of pasta, sauce, meatballs and parmesan and nearly passed out from revulsion. He explained that he needed meatballs separate and far from the pasta, and while he could overlook the sauce on the noodles, parmesan cheese sprinkled haphazardly over the dish was out of the question.

Tobias sat down with a polite smile for my sister. It was hard to tell if he was enamored with my beautiful sister or just afraid of her. She had, after all, had two husbands die off. Though each had one foot in the grave, so to speak, before she even walked down the aisle.

"Toby," Cora started. Just having her say his name nearly caused him to accidentally drop egg into his hash browns. He carefully moved the eggs away from the potatoes.

"Yes, Cora?"

"How do you feel about the new boarder being a man?"

"I suppose I haven't given it much thought. If we're talking ratios, it'll now be even in the house, three men and three women. As long as he's agreeable." Tobias reached for the salt shaker so he could begin his slow destruction of the meal I made him. He tended to shake so much salt on his food, I had purchased him his own personal salt shaker. "Is he an academic, by any chance?" Tobias tended to judge everyone by their level of education. He had three different degrees, all pertaining to numbers and statistics.

His question caused Cora and Opal to laugh behind their hands. We'd made a rule never to laugh at the expense of anyone at the table, but occasionally, a polite, hidden giggle was required.

"What would an academic be doing here on cursed Frostfall Island?" Opal asked. She insisted the island was cursed merely because of the occasional mishap, like the random murder. It was true, statistically speaking, as Tobias might point out, our island had more murders than the average island, but it could hardly be considered cursed. It wasn't as if the island invited murderers to its shores. It was more that murderers just tended to land here.

"What do we know about this new person?" Tobias asked with more interest. He'd finished dousing his eggs and potatoes with salt and could now focus on the conversation.

I sat with my eggs and found myself admittedly ashamed that I didn't know much. "As I said, we've spoken through emails. He said he needed a place to stay. He wanted a quiet place that provided meals. His name is Nathaniel, Nathaniel Smith."

Everyone scoffed at the name Smith, Tobias the loudest. "Unfortunately, Smith is the most commonly used name when someone wants to hide their true identity."

"It's also the most common name period, so the odds are very good that it's his actual name," Cora said. "I like the name Nathaniel. I once dated a Nathaniel. He had the darkest eyes and those arms—" She drifted off for a second, apparently thinking about *those arms*, then she snapped out of her daydream. "I had to break it off with him because it turned out he was married with three kids."

"Good call," Opal said wryly. "Well, let's hope he's interesting. We could use some fresh, new conversation at this table. It's been getting stale lately."

I had sort of tuned out of the table chat. My mind was thumbing back through the few emails I'd received from the new boarder. Had I been too lax? He came with a nice reference from a former landlord. Otherwise, I knew very little about the man.

"Hey, birthday girl," Cora said impatiently. It seemed she'd been trying to get my attention. "Are you walking to the produce stand? I'm off to work."

"Oh right. Yes. I'll walk with you. Our new housemate might be waiting at the ferry stop this morning." Let's hope he doesn't arrive wearing a hockey mask and holding a giant knife, I thought, darkly.

four

MOST OF THE early morning chill had cleared, and the day was pleasant in every respect. Once Cora realized she was no longer supported by rich husbands and still unable to part with her beautiful jewelry, she came to the unavoidable conclusion that she needed an income. Seraphina Butterpond, the owner of Tea, Tarts and Tittle-Tattle, a sweet, marvelous tea room on the touristy edge of town, was a good friend of mine. She hired my sister as a favor. At first, I was in full panic, worried that Cora, with her many eccentricities and utter lack of experience at being anything other than a trophy wife, would fail miserably at the job. Instead, her charm, beauty and extravagant wardrobe had made her a tea room favorite. It worked out for all of us. Sera had a good worker, who attracted customers to the shop. Cora had a purpose and new sense of being productive (instead of spending someone else's money she was earning her own) and I had my needy, attention loving sister out from under my heels while I cooked, shopped and kept the boarding house in running order.

While Cora's wardrobe was always entirely impractical for whatever she was doing, she had taken steps to buy sensible shoes for her walk to work. Bicycling to the tea shop was out of the question. An Alexander McQueen pencil dress was hardly practical for pedaling a bike. Not that Frostfall Island didn't have other modes of transportation, aside from feet and bikes. Many residents preferred getting around on mopeds and electric scooters. A few people even trotted around on horseback, a mode of transportation I always envied, only I lacked both the riding experience as well as the horse. There were a handful of cars and trucks on the island, but it was expensive to have a vehicle brought over from the mainland. There was no gas station, so vehicle owners had to bring fuel over in gas cans. Not that you needed much gas on an island that was only seven miles long and five miles wide. Island Drive was the only paved road on the island, and it could easily be traveled from one end to the other by bike or scooter.

Cora and I stepped off of Island Drive and headed toward Bayberry Harbor. Gulls screeched overhead as some of the fishing boats headed off for their second catch of the day. It was a sight that was always bittersweet for me. It rekindled sorrow, and, at the same time, touched me with sad longing for those early, wonderful days watching Michael head out to sea. I was a glowing newlywed, proud of her husband and excited for whatever adventures awaited us. This morning the gulls were exceptionally energized, lifting and falling, diving and dashing about the vessels as they puttered out past the jetty and the orange buoys.

"What kind of tarts did Sera make today?" I asked.

Cora rubbed her chin in thought. "I think she said she was making those spinach and gruyere cheese savories and raspberry vanilla cream. I forgot the third one."

Sera usually offered two sweet tarts and a savory to go with her vast assortment of teas. She started her place, Tea, Tarts and Tittle-tattle or the 3Ts as we locals called it (even though it was technically four Ts but that topic had been widely debated until we settled on 3Ts because it just sounded better) a year after Michael disappeared. I was lonely and adrift, not sure where to take my life. I'd spent hours in Sera's shop sipping her exotic tea blends and nibbling her tarts, and she would talk to me. No big, sorrowful speeches. No poor, pitiful Anna speeches. Just talk... about everything and anything. It was what I needed. Sera helped me out of a bad funk and, at the same time, became a trusted friend. If not for Sera's friendship and support, I probably would have left the island and never opened the boarding house.

We reached the boardwalk running along the coast. In summer, the same boardwalk that stretched from the Frostfall Historical Society and Maritime Museum on the south to the swimming beach on the north, would be crowded with tourists licking ice cream cones, pedaling tandem bicycles and taking selfies. It was still a little early for the big tourist season, but the boardwalk was bustling nonetheless.

"Sera's expecting a large crowd this morning because of

that silly pirate reenactment event. A bunch of people and a lot of costumes, props and camping equipment came in on the lunchtime ferry yesterday. They set up camp near North Pond." Cora pointed ahead. "See, there's a pirate." The young man dressed in tattered white pants, a striped v-neck shirt and red sash around his waist was handing out flyers for the event, a reenactment of Captain Morgan's battle with Spanish soldiers in the sacking of Portobello.

The reenactment enthusiasts hadn't picked Frostfall randomly. Frostfall had sort of a pirate obsession. A hundred or so years earlier, the locals had convinced themselves that the notorious Caribbean pirates, scoundrels like Blackbeard, Calico Jack and Black Bart, had frequented our humble Atlantic island. They'd created an entire narrative and story, based on little historical evidence, to go with their new theory. It was an attempt to give some character and interesting backstory to their island. A lump of picturesque land with a fishing harbor just wasn't doing it for the early inhabitants. They wanted notoriety like their southern neighbor Ocracoke Island, which could boast, with historical proof, that it was one of Blackbeard's stomping grounds. But the Frostfall folk didn't let lack of evidence stop them. They forged ahead with their farcical narrative, stating emphatically that during the early eighteenth century, long before the harbor was built and the fishing boats had docked, pirates roamed the island, possibly even hiding treasure. None had ever been found but plenty of holes had been dug. One man came to the island with his shovels and gear and ended up digging such a deep hole in his search, he couldn't get out. The locals had to send down a rope to pull him free. Then they made him fill it back up.

Alongside the cast of pirates meandering down the boardwalk, there were a few elegantly dressed Spanish soldiers. They had gone all out on their costumes with snug fitting doublets, frilly, puffy pantaloons and feathered hats.

Cora glanced at her diamond watch. "Darn it. Stopped again." The watch was more valuable than dependable, but it did shine beautifully on her slim wrist. "I think I'm late. Let's pick up the pace."

Sera was just delivering two savory tarts and a pot of tea, chai, if my nose was right, to a Spanish soldier and a woman dressed as a tavern wench, at least that was the persona her bare shouldered peasant dress conveyed. The man looked to be in his forties (I was an expert on that age now since it was in my mirror every morning). His rather smarmy grin was partially hidden by a thick, black moustache that may or may not have been fake. His hair was the same color, so black it was nearly blue in the sunlight streaming past the bright green awning.

Sera's blue eyes sparkled as she looked up from the table. "It's the birthday girl!" Sera was ten years my senior. We'd always had so much in common, it was hard to believe we'd been born in different decades. As far as I could tell, like my sister, Sera had always been stunning. Not in the same classical, magazine cover beauty way as my sister, but in her own unique way. Her hair was raven black, her eyes cerulean blue and her skin was the color of cream, a sort of modern day

Snow White. "I made you a special birthday tart." She motioned toward the tea room. "Do you have time to stop?"

"I always have time for a Seraphina Butterpond tart."

Cora swept inside first to pull on her apron and get started with her work day.

Walking into Sera's shop was like stepping into a mystical daydream. Her eclectic mix of relaxed boho, simple country and fairy tale chic took you to another realm, one where you expected to find tiny, magical fairies with flower hair wreaths and tie dyed wings flitting between the ivy and rose garlands draped along the ceiling and windows. Every chair and table was different, and each one, old and with a story to tell. My favorite was an oak topped stool that twirled on its iron base and had the words *Laramie sat here* etched on the seat. Many times, we debated who Laramie might have been. The final and most agreed upon theory was that he was a cowboy somewhere in Montana who had walked into a saloon and stayed long enough that he decided to leave his mark. There was no basis for the tale of Laramie the cowboy except that the name had a western ring, and Montana seemed the best place for a man named Laramie.

Red check tablecloths and curtains were Sera's homage to her country upbringing, but everything else came from her imaginative mind, a mind that created some of the most unique, tasty tarts in the world, or, at least, on the east coast. And most definitely on Frostfall Island.

Beyond the décor that kept your eyes sweeping around the shop the entire time you sipped tea, the overwhelming fragrance, an earthy, malty base punctuated with pops of spices, cardamom, clove, cinnamon and ginger floated around in clouds. Occasionally, I'd left the shop slightly tipsy from the aroma.

I sat on Laramie's stool and waited as Sera retrieved my special tart from the kitchen. Most of the customers were unfamiliar faces, tourists and people here for the reenactment. The locals came for their tea (mostly the tittle-tattle) after lunch, when tea time was winding down and Frostfall neighbors could sit and chat about things, island things, like the weather, this year's catch and the next delivery of fresh milk to the local market. Sera always knew everything that was going on in town because her shop, literally named for town rumors, was the place everyone came to exchange stories and gossip.

Sera returned, her cheeks red with pride as she carried out a luscious tart. Lemony yellow cream was topped with a crown of glazed blueberries and whipped cream rosettes. "It's lemon and blueberry cheesecake." She placed it in front of me, then turned around and tapped her chin. "Now, which tea to go with it?" She clapped her hands once. "Oolong. I have a new one that has a mellow, buttery flavor." She hurried off to get the tea.

The tart looked incredible. I didn't have the heart to let Sera know that I was already full from breakfast and chocolate covered strawberries. Fortunately, being a good friend, Sera could read it in my expression. She sighed loudly as she returned with the cup of tea. "Let me guess, the Moon River gang already filled you with treats this morning."

I smiled weakly. "Chocolate covered strawberries."

"I'll wrap it to go," she said dejectedly. "But you have to send me a selfie of you eating the tart, and I want to know what you think. I tasted the sample cheesecake batter and it was divine."

"I will record a video of me eating it, complete with sound effects."

"That works. I'll put the tea in a to-go cup."

"You're the best," I said as she walked away.

"I know."

Sera's husband, Samuel, walked in from the back room. "Hey, birthday girl. How are you feeling?" he teased. "I heard it's a big one."

Seraphina's beauty, charm and overall wonderfulness had landed her a young, handsome husband. Even though I was forty now so I could call just about anyone young, Samuel was truly young. Mid-twenties young, which, from my four decade vantage point, seemed almost like childhood. Samuel's shoulders spanned half the counter in front of him, and he had a jaw and cleft chin that could make Kirk Douglas do a double take. Sera met Samuel when she hired him to paint her cottage by the sea. At first, I was ashamed to admit, we were catty about the whole thing, certain that Sera was just having a middle-aged crisis and Samuel was just looking for someone to take care of him. But we were wrong. Samuel turned out to be a doting husband, and Sera looked at him as if he was the greatest man on earth. They were genuinely in love. I had a hard time burying the terrible guilt I felt about jumping in the gossip pool at the start of their relationship.

"Here you go." Sera stared past me as she handed over the

boxed tart and oolong tea. She hopped on her toes to get a view out the window.

I laughed. "What is so interesting out there?" I looked over my shoulder. The Spanish soldier and tavern wench were holding hands over the tiny table.

"They're sure cozy," Sera commented.

I turned back to her. "Those small outdoor tables are perfect for handholding and getting cozy."

"Especially for that conquistador. About an hour ago, he sat at that same table, in that same costume, only then he was holding hands with a different woman. She was definitely not a tavern wench. She had red, wavy hair and no costume. He was drinking black tea. Now he's sipping chai."

I shrugged. "Maybe the elegant, exotic soldier garb has gone to his head." I lifted the box. "Thanks so much, and the video narration of my tart adventure is soon to follow." I waved to Cora on my way out. My birthday had thrown off my schedule. I needed to get to the produce stand before Molly was sold out of potatoes and onions.

five

IN THE DISTANCE, Frannie's *SS Salty Bottom*, heavy with passengers, was making its way back to port. The boat was too far out and the sun too harsh for me to see who was onboard, but there was a good chance Frannie was bringing my new boarder to the island on her morning run. I could hear Molly Pickering's laugh, a melodious, infectious sound, before I'd even passed the ferry boat dock.

Molly's apple cheeks were red from the sun. Even with the massive blue and green checked umbrella shading the produce seller and her wares, Molly always managed to look sunburned. Molly was around fifty, about the same age as Sera, but the two women couldn't have been more different and special in their own ways. I'd never met Molly's husband, Bart. Sadly, he died of cancer ten years earlier. Molly was in despair and ready to give up the produce business to settle back on the mainland. Fortunately, she stayed. I couldn't imagine not having her cheery face and colorful produce to greet me every morning. The grocery store on the island was fine when it came to dairy, crackers, nuts and sundries, but their produce was severely lacking. Since Winston had convinced all of us to go vegetarian for the animals and for our health, fruits and vegetables had become staples. Every day except Sunday, Molly boarded the first ferry out so she could get to the mainland produce market. She was an expert at picking only the tastiest melons, juiciest tomatoes and crispest celery.

Molly was handing off a carton of strawberries to a woman as I reached the stand. Her round baskets, normally brimming with the rich yellows, oranges and reds of nature, were nearly empty. "I figured you'd be late, what with those old bones turning forty and all." Molly winked and laughed before handing me a paper bag, heavy and lumpy with produce. "It's on the house. My birthday treat."

I glanced in the bag filled with potatoes, onions, apples and grapes. "Molly, that's so generous. I don't know how to thank you." I placed my tart box on top of the produce. I was going to return home with quite the haul.

"You can thank me by having the best birthday ever. I remember my fortieth. It was a tough one and then, all of a sudden, I'm looking in the mirror and I'm fifty. Scary stuff but after a few wrinkles and a little chin sagging, I realized I couldn't care less. Each new line or sag is another year that I got through this wonderful adventure called life."

"I need to remember that philosophy, Molly."

A big shadow fell over the produce baskets. "Well, shiver me timbers, look at these wonderful grapes." The man had a booming voice to go with his big barrel tummy and massive height. He tipped his red and gold pirate hat. "Captain Morgan, at your service."

Molly squinted. "Barry Long, is that you under the shade of that hat? Why, of course it is. Anna, I don't know if you've ever met Barry. He has a cute little summer cottage just north of the swimming beach. He only comes here when the weather is nice."

"And when there are pirates afoot." He chuckled. "Nice to meet you, Anna." A long finger pointed out from the giant cuff on his pirate's coat. It was an impressively made red felt coat with gold trim and brass buttons. "You run the Moon River Boarding House, right?"

"Yes, that's me." I nodded. "Nice to meet you. I'm going to assume you're in the reenactment event."

"What reenactment?" he asked with a serious expression. My cheeks warmed as I realized I'd made an embarrassing assumption. Then laughter that was more thunderous than his voice followed. "Yes, I'm part of that silly active role play event. I wasn't going to do it at first, then they offered me lead role as Captain Morgan. Guess I was the only guy who could fit in this costume. I couldn't turn that down."

My phone rang, which was sort of a saved by the bell moment after I'd been duped by a man in a pirate costume. "Nice meeting you, Captain Barry. Thanks for the goodies, Molly. See you later." I pulled the phone out of my pocket. It was my mom. Mom and Dad lived in the city just across the water but in separate houses. They'd been divorced since I was ten. Dad had since remarried. Mom was still very much alone, and there was good reason for that. She tended to be brusque and a little too plain spoken. No filters at all.

I found a sliver of shade provided by a boardwalk sign. "Hi, Mom."

"How is it possible that my baby, my youngest is forty years old?" she almost sounded weepy.

"I assume that's a rhetorical question, unless you need me to explain the birds and the bees and something that must have happened forty years and nine months ago."

"Oh you," she said. "Always trying to get a rise out of me. Well, I'm not taking the bait, especially not on your birthday. Happy birthday, my little sunshine. Though, I guess you're not that anymore. Forty is nothing to sneeze at." She clucked her tongue. "I still can't believe it."

"Is that because I look far too young to be forty, or is it because you look far too young to be the mother of a forty-year-old. In which case, I might remind you that you are also the mother of a forty-six-year-old. Although, Cora's been getting younger instead of older, so maybe you are too."

"My darling Cora. How is she doing all on her own? She just wasn't meant to be alone."

"Cora is doing great. She's happy and working and she's not alone. I've got a household of boarders and, in case you forgot, she's living with her sister."

Now that I'd brought up Cora, the conversation would shift solely to my sister and her woes and widowhood and those dastardly prenups. While my mom had been somewhat supportive when my life was turned upside down by Michael's disappearance, it wasn't nearly the attention and empathy she gave Cora when her husbands died. It wasn't as if two ninety plus men, one on oxygen and the other no longer able to walk on his own, dying was a shocking surprise. But after each death, my mom dropped everything and raced to take care of my sister. Mom came to Frostfall a week after Michael vanished. She made an excuse for the delay, insisting she was sure he'd return, and she didn't want to be in the way during the emotional homecoming. She stayed for a short while but admitted living on an island made her feel antsy. Since having her around was making me feel just as antsy, I was glad to see her go.

"That's right, your collection of oddities." There was that sharp bite I was waiting for.

"They're not odd, they're lovely. How are things with you, Mom?" The surest way to get her to stop dwelling on my life was to ask about hers.

A loud, aggravated sigh coasted through the phone, and I predicted that I was soon going to regret asking about her life. "Well, you know that horrible neighbor, Mrs. Nankin? She insists on putting her trash can on my driveway. She says hers is too steep."

My mom and Mrs. Nankin, a widow, had been enemy neighbors since I could remember. If it wasn't sprinklers getting a car wet, it was a cat using the roses as a bathroom or television sets on too loud. I came to the conclusion years ago that the neighborly feud was something to keep them busy. It was entertainment for both of them.

"I think you should just let her use your driveway. It's wide enough for you to still get out."

"I knew you would side with Mrs. Nankin. You always liked her better than your own mom."

"Her chocolate chip cookies are better than yours, but in all other categories, you win because you are actually my mom and she's just a neighbor."

"Why are her cookies better? Maybe I should try a new recipe."

"I was joking (though not really. Mom's cookies were always dry). I've got to go, Mom. I'm glad you called."

"Give my love to your sister," she chirped out as we hung up.

The produce bag was getting heavy, and the sun was going to melt my delicious tart. I needed to get home, but the distinct fumes of Frannie's ferry were creeping along the boardwalk. It meant she had docked. I was curious to find out whether the new boarder, Mr. Smith, had made the morning crossing.

six

THE *SALTY BOTTOM*'S home port was a splintery, salt-weathered dock that had more loose planks than a seven-year-old had loose teeth. The dock was positioned on the southern end of Bayberry Harbor, a scenic curve of ocean where fishing boats moored between seasons and pleasure boats dropped anchor for a night or two. The Frostfall Hotel, a red roofed building with ivory stucco stretched along much of the harbor beach. The hotel boasted large picture windows on every side, providing unobstructed views of the vivid blue ocean on the west and the lush island landscape on the east. It was a tourist favorite, and they were often booked months in advance. For a fleeting moment, I'd considered opening the house up as a bed and breakfast or casual motel, but the thought of having a non-stop flow of strangers pass through the house just never sat right with me.

Adjacent to the hotel beach, a floating wharf was home to the local bike rental shop, Burt's Bikes, an ice cream kiosk where they served the best rocky road in the east (at least according to their sign) and a fish and chips stand (a particular favorite with the local gulls).

It was a mild day, but Frannie had one of her signature knitted scarves wrapped around her neck like the swirl on a soft serve cone. She liked to knit during her wait times at each dock. Her boat, *SS Salty Bottom*, was always a wonderful sight. Frannie had saved the spry little boat from a tugboat graveyard. *Salty Bottom* was so happy about its reversal of fortune, it never gave Frannie any problems. The thirty foot boat with its flat blue top, rusty tin can middle and barge bottom puttered across the choppy channel six times a day without complaint.

Frannie was sitting on one of the passenger benches eating a banana as I arrived at the boat. "Anna, happy birthday!" She hopped up and disappeared into the wheelhouse a second, then returned with two knitted oven mitts. "I didn't have time to wrap them."

The mitts were purple and lined with a border of bright blue. "They're too pretty to use. Thank you so much."

"You're welcome. It would be all right if you didn't actually use them. Not sure how much protection they provide, and they're not flame proof."

"I'll just hang 'em up, so I can admire them. Uh, Frannie, I was wondering—"

Frannie nodded. "Yes, he came in on this last harbor crossing." Frannie was generally smiling, so when her expression turned grave, I felt a stone drop in my stomach.

"That's not a 'gee, what a great guy' kind of look," I noted.

Frannie's round shoulders lifted and fell with a deep breath. A concerned head shake followed. Now there were two stones in my gut. "I didn't get a good feeling from him, Anna. He was quiet, almost too quiet, if you know what I mean."

"Not really." And I really didn't.

"He was dark and brooding like he had some things on his mind but none of them good."

Frannie, a wife, mother and successful business owner had never been one for drama or theatrics, so I took her concern seriously. What had I done? I'd placed an ad for the room online and in the paper. It had taken over three months for anyone to respond. It made sense considering jobs were scarce on the island, and a morning and evening ferry ride was more of a commute than most people were comfortable with. (Though, it beat sitting on a dead stop highway for an hour any day of the week.) I'd been so thrilled to get an applicant. Had I tossed my usual due diligence out the window? My screening process had been thin at best. Mr. Smith came with a nice letter of reference from his current landlord. He wrote that he had no bad habits, smoking, listening to loud music or staying up all night watching television. I hadn't done a credit check because he paid six months up front. Should that have been a red flag?

I shook off the dozens of negative thoughts. I hadn't even given the man a chance. He said he needed a quiet place to stay and think, and there was no better place for that than the Moon River Boarding House.

"What are you going to do?" Frannie asked, possibly for the second time, but I'd been stuck in my silent freak out.

"I'm going to give him a chance. Maybe he was just having a bad day, or maybe he was seasick," I said with renewed hope. "That's possible. Seasickness can make anyone disagreeable. I assume he was on foot."

Frannie tossed back one of the ends of her scarf. "Yep, with two big bags at his sides. I pointed him in the direction of Calico Trail and told him go north, then you can't miss the boarding house."

"Great. I'll see if I can catch up to him. That way we can have a nice chat before he even reaches the front steps. See you later." I waved the oven mitts. "Thanks again."

It wasn't easy to run with a bag of produce, now made even heavier by a pair of thick, woolen oven mitts. I scooted along the boardwalk and veered off toward the trail. I turned around the large red maple that marked the beginning of the Calico trail. My new boarder was fifty yards ahead. I stopped and watched him for a moment. His thick, dark hair stopped at the collar of his shirt, a dark green t-shirt stretched tightly across his back and broad shoulders. His arm muscles bulged from the heavy bag hanging from each hand. There was something about the way he walked, slow but determined, and, at the same time, a little lost as if he was trying to find his way to something and not just the big Victorian looming over the river ahead.

I watched him walk along the trail with his suitcases, presumably packed with all the belongings he had in the world. Something about the scene in front of me gave me pause. I'd hurried to catch up to him, but my feet now stuck solidly to the ground beneath me and the gap between us widened again. An odd feeling washed over me. Maybe it was just because a complete stranger, a person I'd never seen or, for that matter, spoken with was about to move into the house. It was going to be a big change. I hadn't really thought about it until right then. Things were about to change. Something told me, my life was about to change… profoundly.

seven

JUST SECONDS after my minor meltdown on Calico Trail, I took a deep breath and got my feet moving again. I was jumping to conclusions about our new housemate, and I chided myself for it. Dust kicked up from my short, hurried footsteps. The bag of produce grew heavier in my hand as I scurried ahead.

"Excuse me," I called, but he didn't stop or turn. He kept walking, face forward, his shoulders and back set rigid, like a brick wall. "Excuse me, Mr. Smith?" I asked. Still no response.

I caught up to him. He didn't stop his determined pace, but he did take the time to turn his face toward me. A pair of large eyes gazed at me in a way that was neither friendly nor harsh. They were just there, blue like the ocean surrounding us. I inexplicably tried to decide if his was a gaze I would look forward to seeing over a plate of eggs at breakfast, a game of chess or, for that matter, over a pillow. It wasn't an absolute no. There was something intense, turbulent about his gaze, and I found myself slightly caught up in it, like iron to a magnet. His features were as strong and finely chiseled as his back and shoulders. There was something about his face that assured me he wasn't going to be an easy man to get to know.

"I was calling you," I said. "Didn't you hear me? Or maybe you're not Mr. Smith?"

"You must be Ms. St. James." His face turned forward again. His pace hadn't slowed or hastened. He moved the bags in his hands and shifted his shoulders to rebalance the load.

"Yes, that's me, but you can call me Anna. Should I call you Mr. Smith or Nathaniel?"

He took longer than I would have expected to answer the simple question. "Nate is fine."

"I've got your room all ready. Let me tell you a little bit about the boarding house," I started.

"Just need a room and a place to shower. Like I told you in the emails, I won't be any trouble, and I don't need much. Just a place to get away from civilization."

I paused and looked at him. For the first time, he stopped too and turned to me. I'd already seen his face once, but that didn't stop me from staring at him once again. And this time, he took the opportunity to really look at me. Was he seeing a forty-year-old woman? One who was almost passably pretty in just the right light and shadow? Why did I care? I was spending too much time with my sister. Only she never had to wonder what a man saw when he looked at her. Every time Cora walked into a room, it was that Cinderella moment when she stepped into the ballroom with her incredible dress and glass slippers. I was feeling a little of that at the moment, but instead of seeing Cinderella, the man in front of me, the new stranger who'd just swept in like an unexpected squall, was seeing a hastily dressed, slightly sunburned, somewhat befuddled middle-aged woman. Was forty middle age? Surely not.

I hadn't found my response to his stunning declaration, so he filled in the gap. "Isn't that why you're here?" he asked. "To get away from civilization?" He continued toward the house, leaving me a few steps behind. I caught up to him again, the produce jostling once again in the bag. I'd have nothing more than mashed potatoes and grape juice by the time I reached the kitchen.

"I'm not here to get away from civilization. This is my home. It's the place I feel most comfortable." It wasn't my best work, defense wise, but his arrival had thrown me off balance.

"Exactly. A remote island that I've read has far more birds than people."

"I think that's the case everywhere. I mean, have you ever been in Central Park? There has to be a hundred pigeons to every person. And if you stand out on any beach with a bag of chips—" I was glad to reach the house. It gave me an excuse to stop chattering like a squirrel that had drunk a cup of espresso.

Most people, upon their first visit to the house, stopped to admire its architectural beauty or at least took the time to comment on the general appeal of the place. Nathaniel walked right up the steps, pausing only to wipe his shoes on the welcome mat. As we both rid ourselves of trail dust, the door swung open.

Not expecting us on the other side, Tobias startled. "Anna, there you are. I just came back. I forgot my lunch." He spoke to me but stared at Nathaniel. "Is this Mr. Smith?" Tobias opened the screen door, and while trying to hold it open, awkwardly stuck out his hand only to realize the new boarder didn't have a hand free for a shake. Tobias quickly withdrew his hand, and the screen door snapped shut. He nodded. "Nice to meet you. I'm Tobias." He then gathered some composure, opened the screen and held it for both of us.

"Nate," Nathanial muttered curtly and strolled past toward the stairs.

Tobias looked hurt and a little miffed. Not much angered the man unless he'd had a particularly bad day at work where numbers weren't adding up right. I smiled sheepishly at Tobias and gave him a friendly wink.

Tobias cleared his throat and straightened his gray tie. "Yes, well, I'm off to work. I'll see you later."

Nathaniel was polite enough to stop at the bottom of the stairs, but I presumed that was only because he didn't know how to find his room.

"Turn right at the top, then it's the second door on the left," I said. "I'll show you the way if you just let me set down the produce."

"No need. Those directions work."

"Right. Let me know if there's anything you need. The men's bathroom is just across the hallway, with the black and white tile and round mirror. There are towels in your closet. By the way, lunch is at half past twelve. And dinner at six. We always make a point of eating together at the big pine table whenever we're home."

"I'll take my meals in my room if you don't mind."

Once again, I was dumbstruck. "Fine," I eventually sputtered out. "But you'll have to pick up your plate in the kitchen."

"No problem." He climbed up the stairs with his heavy suitcases, turned right and never looked back once.

Oh, Anna, what have you done?

eight

EVENING HAD SETTLED on the island and on my fortieth birthday. I pulled my sweater closer as Huck and I stood by the river. Spring melt was flowing down from Calico Peak, the one mountain on the island, though, at two thousand feet above sea level, it was more just a glorified hill. Moon River flowed down from the peak, growing in size and energy as the frosted tip of the mountain finally shed its layers of winter snow. The river nearly cut the island in two before emptying into the ocean on the southern tip. Small bridges were a necessity, especially in spring when the river was full of life. The mossy smell of the river always let me know I was home. It permeated nearly every corner of the yard and front porch.

Huck turned toward the house. Yellow light, laughter and the aroma of oregano spilled from the kitchen windows. In yet another shock for the day, my sister had insisted I leave dinner entirely in her hands. Of course, by her hands, she meant Seraphina's hands. During the workday, the two had concocted a plan for lasagna and Sera's delicious mocha flecked cake. It was a cake with a hint of malt and coffee. Each scrumptious bite contained dark flecks of chocolate and curls of chocolate were piled high on the pillowy buttercream frosting. Just the anticipation of the cake and lasagna with all my friends had erased some of the angst I was feeling about the new tenant.

Nathaniel had come down to pick up his lunch plate. At some point, while I was outside watering the rose bushes, he returned the plate. I hadn't seen or heard him the rest of the day. Opal had been at home all day, mostly in her room watching a Doris Day marathon, but she had not crossed paths with Nathaniel once. Only Tobias had met him, and it was brief and frosty. Was it possible a youngish man would spend his entire day locked up in the room of his boarding house, talking to no one and not even venturing out of doors? Cora had been trying to pry information out of me, but I really had nothing to say. It was almost as if I'd just walked a complete stranger into the house and up to a spare bedroom. On second thought, that was exactly what I'd done.

Frannie and Molly's voices pulled my attention to the trail. "There's the birthday girl," Frannie chirruped. "I heard rumor that Sera was making her famous mocha fleck cake for this special occasion."

I hugged both of them. "Thanks for coming, and yes, you heard right. I was shooed out of the house earlier, but I think we can head back inside. It's getting a little cold out here, and I'm dying to see what's going on in my kitchen."

"You've got nerves of steel," Frannie said. "I can't stand it when someone else cooks in my kitchen. Especially the kids. Puts my teeth on edge. They never put things back in the right place, and I'm not sure why but there's always a sticky mess on the counter. Even when nothing sticky has been made, it stills seems as if someone smeared a cloth with maple syrup and wiped it all over the counter."

Molly smiled broadly. "Well, with that little pep talk to put your mind at ease, let's go inside and see what's happening."

Frannie was able to fire off two quick questions before we reached the house. "How was the new guy? Did you get the same bad vibes?"

Molly's face flashed my direction. "Bad vibes? New guy? Anna, did you meet someone?"

"What? No. I have a new boarder, and Frannie got bad vibes." That was all I said. I wasn't going to let Frannie know that I was worried too. Mostly because I wasn't sure if the vibes were bad or just a little out of sorts. The rest of the boarders, even with their eccentricities, had all fit snugly into the group. We got along well, respected each other and were glad for the companionship. It didn't take a genius to conclude that Nathaniel wasn't going to fit in any of the aforementioned categories.

"Something is burning," Frannie said as we walked into the kitchen. Tobias was filling glasses with ice water. Winston was still upstairs putting his baby robins to bed.

Sera looked up from the cake stand where she was piling chocolate curls onto the frosting. "Cora, you were in charge of watching the garlic bread. I warned you it burned easily."

Cora had been scrolling through her phone. She dropped it into the pocket on the apron she had wrapped around her shimmering blue dress. "Oops, forgot all about it." She opened the oven, and the four of us shouted simultaneously.

"Use oven mitts!"

Cora laughed airily. "I know that. I just forgot them, that's all." She grabbed the mitts from the hook and pulled out a slightly smoky pile of garlic bread. A luscious tray of cheesy lasagna sat on a cooling rack waiting to be served. It was instinctual for me to start putting food on plates. I picked up the knife and spatula.

Sera was still working on perfecting the cake. She glanced up. "Cora, you're supposed to serve the lasagna so Anna can relax."

Cora stared down at her snug fitting dress. "This is a Helmut Lang original. I don't want to get sauce on it."

"It's all right, Cora. Have a seat. I don't mind serving. After all, you both did all the work." I winked secretly at Sera to let her know I knew she did all the work and that my sister was probably more trouble than help.

I was concentrating on slicing perfect squares in the layers of cheesy goodness and had not noticed someone new had joined the crowd in the kitchen, a crowd that had gone utterly silent. It was the sudden quiet that alerted me to Nathaniel's arrival. All eyes were glued to the new tenant. A few chins had dropped as well, especially Cora's. Nathaniel had changed to a white t-shirt and jeans.

For any normal person, it would have been that horrible, awkward first day at a new school where the entire class falls silent to stare at the new kid. And stare my dear friends did. In fact, a little gawking and ogling were sprinkled in as well. Nathaniel wasn't the least bit put off by the stir he had caused or, in this case, un-stir since everyone appeared to be frozen in time.

Nathaniel nodded slightly and motioned toward the cake before turning his deep blue gaze toward me. "Is it someone's birthday?"

"It's Anna's," Cora chirped. She pulled herself out of her trance faster than everyone else. She'd had more experience than most women with very attractive men, and Nathaniel was definitely that.

Nathaniel looked up at the silver balloons hanging from the garland. They'd started to droop and looked a little sad and deflated. "Your twenty-fifth?"

Cora's loud burst of laughter startled everyone. "She's forty," she said quickly and unnecessarily. "I'm her sister."

"Yes, my older sister," I added, deciding she deserved it.

"We're having a little celebration," Sera said. "Pull up a chair."

"No, thanks." He picked up a plate of lasagna, a piece of garlic bread and a glass of water. "I'll bring these back down when I'm done." Then, just as unceremoniously as he'd arrived, he turned and left. He stopped in the doorway and glanced back. Everyone was still gawking at him, but that didn't seem to bother him at all. His gaze landed right on me again. There was a long moment where he just looked at me. "Happy birthday, Anna." He turned and left.

Everyone at the table waited for his footsteps to ascend the stairs and for his bedroom door to shut before breaking into a frenzied conversation.

Tobias, who never spoke loudly, was the first to comment… and loudly. "Very rude. Never seen such terrible manners."

I put a finger to my lips. "Keep it down. This house has thin walls." I wasn't going to stop them from talking about the new boarder because I wanted to hear their opinions. I already knew Frannie's, and the scowl on her face reinforced it. She didn't like the man but then she didn't live at Moon River, so her opinion wasn't a crucial one.

I was hoping for some constructive first impressions from the other women in the house, but staying true to form, my sister and Opal launched into a debate about his appearance.

Opal was still staring at the empty space where Nathaniel had just been standing. Then, she spun back to face the table. "If Clark Gable and Ava Gardner had a love child, it would be that man." She sat back confidently in her bright pink dress as if she had just solved the mysteries of the universe.

"No, no." Cora wiped the lipstick from the corner of her mouth and sat forward with self-importance, letting everyone know she was about to say something noteworthy. "If Brad Pitt and George Clooney had a love child—"

I laughed before she could finish. "How does that work exactly? Which one is giving birth, Brad or George?"

Cora waved her bright pink fingernails. "That's just semantics."

Tobias was rarely impolite, especially when it came to my sister, but even he couldn't hold back a laugh. "Actually, I believe that's science."

"What's science?" Winston asked as he walked into the kitchen. He didn't wait for an answer because the aromas and sights in the kitchen had grabbed his full focus. "Oh wow, Cora, did you make that lasagna? It smells delicious."

Cora shrugged as if it had been nothing at all, a simple meal to prepare. "Thanks. Sera helped." Once again Sera and I exchanged secret friend glances. "We were just discussing the new boarder," Cora filled Winston in.

"Oh yeah, that guy. We passed each other in the hallway earlier." That was all Winston had to say, and that was not at all like Winston. Everyone waited for him to elaborate. Instead, he picked up a piece of garlic bread and put it on his plate.

I decided to prod further. "Did he introduce himself, or were you just left to wonder whether a stranger was wandering around the house?"

Winston had tried to comb down his thick head of blond hair, but, as usual, his attempts had failed. It was like a giant, puffy yellow cloud on his head. "You told me we were getting a new boarder. I just assumed that the dark, brooding guy trudging across to the bathroom was the new guy. Not very friendly," he added. "But I knew guys like that in high school and always learned to just walk a wide berth around them."

Tobias tapped the table, a little more loudly than he

planned, apparently, because he looked somewhat embarrassed about the clamor. "See, that is my opinion. He is someone to be avoided." Tobias adjusted his glasses on his nose as he turned a serious frown my direction. "He sure doesn't seem suited for the Moon River Boarding House."

I handed Tobias his specially made plate of plain lasagna noodles with a dollop of ricotta cheese and a bowl of marinara on the side. He immediately picked up his personal salt shaker to begin his salting ritual. Sera knew all about his salt obsession along with his aversion to eating foods that were mixed together, but she still frowned at him as if insulted.

I sat next to Opal. She had just finished topping her plate with parmesan. "I think we all need to give the man a chance. He might just be shy or not used to living with strangers. He'll warm up." She plucked up a piece of garlic bread. "Or... he might be a serial killer. Hard to know for sure." Her red lipstick stretched into a broad grin. She just tossed that zinger out, then picked up her wine glass. "Now, how about a toast for the birthday girl? To our Anna."

All glasses were raised. "To our Anna."

I smiled and sipped my wine, pretending to be in the birthday spirit, but my mind kept slipping back to the phrase *serial killer*.

nine

I BRISKLY STIRRED THE EGGS. It turned out lasagna, cake and worry about my new tenant was the perfect recipe for a restless night. I'd slept right through my predawn alarm and would have slept through breakfast if Huck hadn't finally pounced on the bed to wake me.

My entire schedule was off, so I was feeling utterly out of sorts. My early morning watercolor in nature session was like my first cup of coffee. It cleared my head and allowed me to shuffle my mental to-do list into order. Without it, my day was going to be busy and scrambled like the yellow liquid I was pouring into the hot pan. The eggs sizzled over the layer of bubbling butter. On top of starting breakfast late, Opal and Winston had gotten up extra early.

Opal insisted she never needed to sleep late. She blamed it on being sixty, but I was sure it had more to do with her going from a busy classroom teacher to a classic movie binger. She hardly moved all day except to come down to breakfast or take a stroll around outside the house. On those rare outings, she'd dawn a flowing, floral print moomoo and wide brimmed straw hat, then, with chin lifted, she'd glide around the yard like Greta Garbo walking dramatically onto a movie set. Winston, on the other hand, had two reasons to be up early. His two semi-feathered buddies wanted food at the crack of dawn, and Winston was on early morning feeding duty at the sanctuary.

Lost in my thoughts about the day ahead, my newest occupant and life in general, I was only half listening to the conversation behind me.

"She'd never bother with someone like me," Winston lamented. I knew, without having to pay too much attention, he was talking about Alyssa, the woman who ran the sanctuary. She seemed to be someone who was so involved and consumed by her job, she had no time for a social life. Winston had a huge crush on the woman. I could only imagine how hard it would be fall in love with someone you had to work closely with everyday and not be able to confess those feelings. But Winston worried the crush was very much one-sided, and if he let Alyssa know how he felt, he might lose his job. It was a valid concern.

"I think you should ask Alyssa out and don't dawdle. When I was Valentino, if I saw a woman I admired, I jumped right to it. Be bold."

"I'm not Rudolph Valentino," Winston said dejectedly. "If I were, I'd have already asked her to marry me."

Opal laughed. "Well, we can't all be Valentino. But, Anna, what do you think? Shouldn't he ask Alyssa out, possibly to that ridiculous pirate spectacle? That's a nice, casual place to start."

I spun around with two plates of eggs and nearly dropped both of them. Nathaniel was standing in the doorway, casually leaning against the doorjamb, waiting, apparently, for his breakfast. Opal and Winston were equally surprised to see him, which confirmed my observation that he moved quietly, like a cat in fluffy socks. And it wasn't an easy feat on the creaky wooden floors.

"Oh, Mr. Smith, I mean, Nate, I'll have your food right up."

His mouth turned up at one corner. "No hurry. Just listening to the conversation." Right then, Tobias sidled past Nate without even a cursory nod. Tobias sat at his spot on the table, placed his napkin on his lap and put his hands primly in that same lap. His thin lips were curled in, which seemed to indicate he had nothing to say. Poor Tobias had gotten a rude brush off from our new family member, and it seemed he was taking it quite personally. I delivered Tobias's special plate, eggs with two biscuits placed far enough apart on the dish so there was no cross contamination of biscuit with egg. He set right to work showering the food with salt, a habit that did not go unnoticed by the man in the doorway. I wondered how much of the conversation Nathaniel overheard. He was getting the full scope of our unique family.

"Nate, I don't think I introduced you to two of our other tenants, Winston Katz and Opal Barlow. Everyone, this is Nathaniel Smith."

"So nice to see you again," Cora practically sang the words

from behind. Like Tobias, she sidled past him but with more swing of the hips. She made sure to brush his arm as she passed. My sister was wearing a low-cut, slinky black dress and six inch heels, an even more impractical than usual outfit for a day of work in the tea house. I was sure she had our new tenant in mind when she picked her wardrobe this morning. Cora held out her long, thin hand and graced him with a smile that I used to call her devilishly coy smile, one she used on boys in the neighborhood when she wanted them to buy her an ice cream or ask her to a dance. The way she held her hand, flopped at the wrist and dangling limply in the air, meant she expected a kiss on the back of her hand. My sister ignored all societal norms when it came to meeting men.

Nathaniel left her hand dangling as he nodded his hello. Silent nods seemed to be his favorite communication mode. After an awkward pause, Cora lowered her hand and pulled her heavily glossed lips tight. She turned sharply on her high heels and stomped to her spot at the table.

The whole room was now tense with uncomfortable silence. Winston, the least affected by it, continued to shovel in his breakfast. Opal had a somewhat amused grin on her face as she generously buttered her biscuit. She and Cora were friends, but there was always a slight competition between them. I just wasn't exactly sure what they were competing about. Tobias ate his salty eggs demurely as if he was being judged on his table manners. While he was normally rather quiet at the table, compared to the rest of us, he didn't spare even a glance toward anyone else. Cora, still stinging from a rare male rejection, stabbed at her soft boiled egg with a fork, obliterating the shell and making it inedible. On the other hand, Nathaniel, the catalyst for the strained breakfast atmosphere, stood relaxed in the doorway, arms lightly crossed and a hint of a grin. He seemed to be enjoying the discomfort he had caused in the room.

I hastened his breakfast, tossing a large scoop of eggs and three buttered biscuits onto a plate. I held out the plate, and he padded quietly into the kitchen. Our eyes met over the pile of scrambled eggs. His thick hair was brushed back off his face. His gaze stuck to my face. I held the dish just a little longer than necessary.

"There's coffee on the sideboard." I motioned to the antique pine sideboard on the back wall of the kitchen.

He stared down at his plate. "No bacon or sausages?"

The silence in the room seemed to get even quieter when forks stopped moving. All faces popped up. "All the meals at the boarding house are vegetarian. I mentioned it in my emails. If it's a deal breaker—"

"Not a deal breaker, just asking." He nodded to the table and walked out with his breakfast. Again, the silence held until his bedroom door shut.

Tobias released a breath he must have been holding. "I don't see how this can go on for six months."

Cora's mouth was pulled down as she halfheartedly ate a biscuit. She had nothing to add.

Opal tilted her head side to side. "Not a great start for the new tenant, I'm afraid. I thought the lack of bacon might cause him to go upstairs and pack."

I looked at Winston to see what he thought. "Don't know why he can't be a little friendlier. He's definitely different. I'm with Tobias. Six months is a long time."

I blew out a long, discouraged sigh. "I'm sorry, guys. Looks like I made a mistake. Still, let's give him a chance. Maybe he'll come around."

"Or maybe he'll kill us all in our sleep," Opal said calmly before taking a bite of biscuit.

ten

MY BASKET WAS heavy with eggs, this morning's biscuits, a bar of dark chocolate, apples and two of the banana nut muffins I baked after breakfast. Olive Everhart lived on the east side of the island. Her cedar shingled cottage overlooked Thousand Step Beach, a scenic strip of silky, ivory sand on the farthest eastern edge of the island. To reach the nice little swath of coast, you had to descend six sets of wooden stairs. It wasn't exactly a thousand steps, although it felt like it on the way back up. Olive, a fifty-something artist, lived alone in her charming little house. Anxiety and a touch of agoraphobia meant she rarely left home, so I delivered a basket of food to her house whenever I had time.

"Huck!" I called as I stepped outside with my basket of goodies. I added in a whistle and waited to see the dog trot up from the river or out of the wilderness area behind the house, but there was no sign of him. I decided to start my journey, certain he would catch up to the scent of my basket before too long.

I crossed the bridge and stopped to look over the railing just in case the silly dog had stranded himself on a rock. Still no sign of him. I left the bridge and turned onto Chicory Trail, a narrow path that led directly to Thousand Step Beach and Olive's cottage. I wasn't far along the trail when I spotted my wayward dog… and his new friend… apparently.

Nathaniel was jogging toward me. His shirt and forehead were wet with sweat. Huck trotted steadily next to him as if they'd been running partners for years. I couldn't remember the last time the dog had stuck by my side on a walk or hike.

It was a slightly brisk morning and the ocean breeze was particularly biting, but Nathaniel didn't seem to mind. I wondered whether he'd just keep jogging right past, possibly pausing for one of his curt, non-committal nods. Surprisingly, he stopped.

"I guess I should have told you I borrowed your dog. Actually, he sort of invited himself along for the run." Huck sat obediently at Nathaniel's feet and gazed up at the man with admiration.

"I hope you don't mind that he tagged along. He doesn't usually warm up to people this fast." Maybe that was a good sign, I thought. Animals were always the best judge of character. Surely, Huck would sense if something was amiss with the newest household member. Wouldn't he? Or maybe Huck just felt like a run since we'd missed our pre-dawn outing.

Nathaniel leaned down to pat Huck's head. He'd already lavished far more attention on Huck than on any of the people in the house. Cora had left after breakfast looking as if a lover had jilted her after Nathaniel ignored her proffered hand.

I lifted my basket. "Just taking some food to a friend. She lives at the end of this trail."

"I need to cool down. Mind if I walk with you?"

I was so stunned by his offer, I didn't say yes right away.

"Or not," he said. "I can make my way back."

"No, please walk with me." We started along the path. The view out to the ocean was one of those crystal clear ones, where you were sure if you looked hard enough you could see all the way to tomorrow. White crests topped the ripples, and a group of gulls had found something of interest, a school of fish most likely, in the waves. "What do you think of the island so far?"

He gazed out at the water. "I can see why you want to live here. It not only takes you away from civilization, it takes you away from all the chaos, noise and pollution on the mainland."

I looked over at him. "I'm not avoiding civilization. I just happen to prefer the people surrounding me to the general population."

A line formed on the side of his mouth as he smiled briefly. "You do surround yourself with interesting people."

"They're wonderful," I said briskly.

"Didn't say they were bad people. I said they were interesting." He reached up and raked back his hair. "I've got to ask—does—the woman with red hair, Opal?" He turned to me to see if he'd remembered the name.

I nodded. "Yes, Opal and yes, she firmly believes that in a past life she was Rudolph Valentino."

"I see." He didn't laugh or roll his eyes. That was a check in the plus column. That, along with my dog's reaction. Huck was walking right next to him and rather than running off to chase the chickadee that was sitting in the center of the trail, he gazed up at his new friend.

"One night, Opal had a dream," I began, "a very vivid one. In the dream she was sitting on a movie set with Charlie Chaplain. Then someone handed her a mirror, and Rudolph Valentino was staring back at her. She woke up and decided from that moment on that she had been Valentino in a previous life."

Nathaniel reached up and rubbed the dark stubble on his chin, trying to process the whole thing. "I once had a really clear dream about Moby Dick."

He was making light of it now, but in general he'd handled the whole thing well considering it was somewhat absurd.

"That does not mean you were Captain Ahab in a former life," I noted.

He shook his head. "Actually, I was thinking that I might have been the whale in a former life. Nah, scratch that. I prefer to think that big white whale is still swimming around out there terrorizing whaling boats."

I laughed. "You do realize we're talking about a fictional whale, right?"

Nathaniel's blue eyes peered my direction. They were

shadowed by dark lashes. "How do you know we're not all living a fictional life right now?"

"Nope, not going to fall into that philosophical rabbit hole. I'm living a real life, thank you very much."

He laughed. It was brief but I still managed to hear it. I wondered if I would hear more of it. We walked in silence for a second before he broke it with one word.

"Vegetarian?" he asked.

"There's a story to go with it." We were reaching the end of the trail and nearing Olive's cottage. I was sort of sorry to come to the end of our walk. I stopped and, unlike the day before when he kept right on going, he stopped too. "You might have noticed that Winston is carrying around two baby birds in a pouch."

"I did. However, after prioritizing my questions about the other tenants, the Rudy V. thing came to the top, even over the salt habit. I didn't want to seem nosy."

"Makes sense. Winston works at the Wildlife Rescue on the northern tip of the island. He brings home animals that need around the clock care, like the baby robins. One day, he brought home two brand new baby lambs. Their mother had died giving birth. The lambs were going to be put down, so the rescue took them in. We all fell madly in love with little Bubbles and Cuddles. They'd jump into our laps and wait to be snuggled. Even Tobias allowed a little lap time, which was entirely out of character. One evening, while we were all enjoying the two little lambs as they hopped around the kitchen, I pulled out the lamb chops I'd been marinating for dinner. We all just stared at the chops for like five minutes, no one saying a word. I picked up the tray and tossed it into the trash. Everyone clapped and we made a pact right then to go vegetarian. I'm sorry you didn't notice it in the email. I can give you a refund if—"

He shook his head. "No, it's fine. Although, it does seem as if you're trying to get rid of me."

"No, no, not at all. I'm—I'm sorry if you feel that way. This is just a change for everyone in the house and for me." I turned my face toward the breeze to cool my cheeks of the embarrassing blush. "I just love a walk. They say walking is good for the soul. Don't you agree?"

Nathaniel stared down at the ground, then lifted his face to mine. His deep blue eyes seemed to be conveying a lot of thoughts, but I wasn't expecting the one that tumbled out. "My soul took a walk long ago, and it never came back."

I was left speechless by his statement and had no time for a response.

"Anna! Anna!" Olive was waving from her front stoop. I waved back.

"Lunch will be ready at half past noon," I said as I turned back to him. Our previous conversation had officially ended with his zinger.

"Great. Should I take Huck back with me?" he asked.

Huck was glued to his side. "I think he's planning on it."

Without another word, he walked back along the trail, my faithful dog trotting by his side. For a second, it felt like things were moving forward. I was starting to feel more at ease with the new housemate, but his dark comment had taken me right back to square one.

eleven

OLIVE HAD HER LONG, wavy hair pulled up in a scarf. She waved me quickly inside as if just briefly standing on her front stoop was long enough to be out of the house. Olive's quaint A-frame cottage with its cedar shingles, shake roof and earthy green shutters looked more like it belonged on some windswept prairie rather than overlooking the Atlantic Ocean. Olive had purchased the house from an elderly couple who left the island when the cold and damp was becoming too much for their joints.

"I've made some tea," Olive said.

"Perfect and I brought some banana nut muffins." We walked through the tiny front room and straight into the postage stamp sized kitchen. Small as it was, the design was practical, and Olive had plenty of space for storage and cooking. The wall behind her tiny kitchen table, just big enough for two people and two cups of tea, was dotted with an array of her paintings. Olive called herself a numerical painter, a fancy phrase for her paint by number masterpieces. Surprisingly, she sold her artwork and had a big following online. Some of the more snooty artists liked to taunt her and call her a cheat. While it was a bit of a con selling artwork that came in a kit, Olive was quite skilled at it. After all, how often did an amateur artist have a paint by number come out just like the photo on the box? I vaguely remembered a few attempts as a child, the sad-eyed puppy and the tilted head kitten. My finished products were disappointing to say the least.

From the small art studio in the back, a screeching voice sang out the first few lines of 'Sympathy for the Devil' from the Stones. Olive set a cup of tea in front of me and pulled up a chair. "Johnny has been singing that one all morning. It came on the radio while I was painting. Couldn't turn it off fast enough. It's one of his favorites, but I don't care for it."

Johnny, a twenty-year-old scarlet macaw, was nicknamed the Rock and Roll Parrot by Olive's followers. The bird had an impressive repertoire of songs he could belt out at a simple request. He only knew a line of the chorus or, in the case of his current song, the iconic first line, but he kept in tune and considering he was a bird, it was pretty impressive. I was fairly certain Johnny's singing videos were the reason for Olive's big following. Everyone wanted to own a piece of art painted by the woman who lived with the Rock and Roll Parrot.

Olive pulled the muffins out of the basket. "Mmm, these smell good."

"None for me, Olive. I've got more at home. The tea is good."

She placed a muffin on a napkin and pulled out the second chair. "So, Anna, who was that nice looking man you were talking to on the trail? I've never seen him before."

"That's my new tenant, Nathaniel Smith." My mind went straight back to our conversation. It started lighthearted enough but went dark fast.

Olive reached across to take my hand. "Something is on your mind," she prodded.

I smiled weakly. "It's just that I was so glad to finally have someone answer my ad for the room, I rushed and accepted his application. Not sure if he's a good fit for the house. Some of the others have taken a disliking to him. Nate's fault really. He hasn't made any effort to give a good impression. The opposite in fact. He's been cold and aloof."

Olive sat back with her tea. There was a small smudge of green paint just below her hairline. I was so used to seeing her with paint smears, it would have seemed weird for the smudge not to be there. "I'm sensing some mistrust too."

"Yes, all due to my rush to get a boarder in that room. I would never forgive myself if I'd willingly invited someone with nefarious motives into the house."

The lines in Olive's face softened to concern. "I can tell this has you worried."

Olive was always my sounding board. She knew what I was thinking sometimes even before I knew it.

"I'm not sure if I'm worried or not. It's like that tiny rock you get in your shoe while you're walking. It bothers you and you know it's there and you should probably stop and shake it out. Then it slips somewhere and you can't feel it for a few steps so you push the bother from your mind. Then, all of a sudden, it's back. That's how I'm feeling about Mr. Smith. Does that make sense?"

"It does." She nibbled a piece of muffin. "Hmm, yummy. Now, here's my two cents and it's probably not even worth that. You're an investigator. That ridiculous detective they send from the mainland—what's his name? Norwich or Inspector Clouseau as we so *lovingly* call him, is worthless. All of the murder cases on this island would have gone unsolved or with the wrong person in jail if not for you. Why don't you put on your investigator's cap and do a little snooping. It's not too late. It's better to be ahead of the problem than behind it."

I picked up my tea. "You're right, Olive. It's not like me to just sit back and let the proverbial chips fall where they may. I'm going to do some digging. I owe it to my Moon River family." I sipped the tea and sighed. "I always feel better after I've talked to you, Olive."

"Squawk, talk to Olive. Squawk!" Johnny flew into the room and landed gently on the back of Olive's chair. She handed him a crumb of muffin, and he dropped to the floor to eat it.

We both watched him eat the treat. "Nature produces so many amazing colors, but I think she really outdid herself with scarlet macaws," I said.

"I couldn't agree more." Olive reached down and stroked Johnny's head. He instantly went into his imitation of a cat purr, something he was apt to do when stroked. While it sounded a little more throaty than the purr of a cat, there was no mistaking it.

I drank the rest of my tea. "Well, I should get home. I've got a little research to do. I think I'll start on Google."

"Good idea but with a name like Smith," Olive started, then looked at me. "Do you think that's his real name?"

"See, that should have been the first red flag, yet I blithely invited him to live at Moon River. What was I thinking?"

"Squawk! What was I thinking?" Johnny repeated.

Olive smiled apologetically. "He's beautiful, brilliant and slightly annoying."

twelve

MOST OF THE shops in town had closed after lunch so people could get ready to attend the pirate spectacle at North Pond. Cora and Opal finished their lunches and went upstairs to change. Winston and Tobias were still at work. Nathaniel picked up his grilled cheese sandwich and lemonade and once again disappeared into his room. I took the few moments of quiet and solitude in the kitchen to do some research.

I pushed aside my grocery list and opened my laptop. I typed in the name Nathaniel Smith. Smith might have been as common as moths, but Nathaniel was not. At least that was what I thought until eight million results popped up when I typed in the name. I added United States and Rhode Island, the closest state, to the keywords and hardly narrowed down the results at all. Each entry I opened talked about a Nathaniel Smith, but none of them matched my Nathaniel Smith.

I slumped back. "Needle meet haystack," I muttered. I was starting to get the feeling that, just like everyone mentioned, Smith was the go-to name people used when they didn't want to be found or caught. "The previous landlord." I searched through my email correspondences and found the attached letter from Trevor Jones, the landlord of the Riverside Apartments where Nathaniel lived. Mr. Jones had signed off with a phone number in case I had questions. His letter had gone on about how neat and quiet Mr. Smith was and how he was never late on rent and courteous to the other tenants. All seemed in order so I'd never considered making a call. Another regret.

I dialed the number and was surprised (yet not that surprised) to find the number belonged to a Pet Mart. Wasn't Jones the name people used when they decided not to go with Smith? How could I have been so careless? He'd even used names that should have clued me into his whole scam.

The clunking pipes in the walls let me know someone had turned on the water in the men's bathroom. Nathaniel was taking a shower. A new idea struck me, one that terrified me, but, at the same time, seemed more than reasonable considering what I'd just discovered about the glowing letter of reference. I'd placed my good friends in danger, and now, I needed to right that stupendous wrong.

My heart pounded as I climbed the stairs. A good case of nerves was the last thing I needed right then, but I'd never conducted an investigation inside my house. And I'd certainly never searched a boarder's room and belongings. I wasn't sure what I was looking for, but, as always, when I was investigating, I'd know it when I found it.

The shower was still running as I crept past the bathroom. I knocked lightly on the bedroom door. There was no answer. He never brought down his dishes. I would use that as an excuse if I was lame enough to get caught. But I didn't plan on it. I pushed the key into the lock and opened the door.

Nathaniel's bags had been unpacked. His clothes were put away in the closet and dresser. I considered it a good sign. If he was about to murder everyone in the house, he'd want to make a fast getaway. That grim thought sent a shiver through me.

The running shoes Nathaniel was wearing when I met him on the trail this morning were sitting next to the dresser. The only thing on top of his dresser was a walnut handled hairbrush. Something about the lone brush with no other belongings, nothing else to define the man, pushed a dull ache of loneliness through me. It was a feeling I hadn't experienced in a long time, but the sight of the hairbrush and a room mostly austere and void of belongings had somehow kicked it back into gear. But the loneliness I felt wasn't mine. It was his. The whole thing gave me pause. Why was I snooping in this lonely man's room? What was he trying to escape? Was he dangerous or just heartbroken by something that had happened? I knew, too well, how badly heartbreak could turn your life upside down.

One thing that stood out in the room, the one item that seemed out of place in the otherwise mostly empty room was a file folder sitting on the nightstand. I still heard the shower, but my time was limited. I tiptoed quickly across the room to the folder, a simple manila one with the letters PTK hastily written on top.

My feelings of guilt about snooping quickly dissipated when I casually flipped it open. It was a collection of newspaper articles, cut neatly out of the paper. A breath struggled to get free from my chest. I could hear my heartbeat in my ears as I thumbed through the articles, each one from a different paper, different journalist but each one covering the same topic, the Pillow Talk Killer. Being out on the island kept us from some of the mainstream horrors in the news, but the serial killer, labeled the Pillow Talk Killer because he covered his victim's heads with a pillowcase and left love notes in lipstick, had been in and out of the local news for six or seven years. The madman or woman had never been caught. Time would pass and those of us not involved with the victims would easily forget about the monster, then all of a sudden a new victim, always a woman, would be found, and the nightmare would start again. Even with my interest in murder mysteries, I hadn't paid much attention to the case. Those murders were happening on the mainland, not here on our wonderful island. It was easy enough to put off any concern or fear… until now. Why would Nathaniel Smith be interested enough in the case to collect newspaper articles? Unless, of course, the articles were about him.

"Find what you're looking for?" a deep voice drawled from behind.

I gasped and flipped the folder shut so forcefully several

of the clippings popped out and fluttered to the floor. "I was just—" I swung around and gasped again. A towel was wrapped low around Nathaniel's hips. Other than the irritated scowl on his face, he wasn't wearing anything else. My startled gaze floated across his chest, muscular and tanned. It was impossible not to notice the deep round scar just below his clavicle. Was it a bullet hole?

"I was looking for the lunch dishes," I sputtered. It was such a clumsy excuse. I felt the color come back to my face in a warm, embarrassed blush.

He moved closer. I stepped back but my legs bumped into the nightstand. He was near enough with that naked chest and that unusual scar that I could see beads of water in the hollow of his throat.

"I took the dishes down earlier. You were at your desk on the computer. I didn't want to disturb you, so I just placed them in the sink."

"How?" I was flabbergasted again. "You move so quietly." I had no idea why I brought it up right then, but it had stuck in my mind. Stealthy, like a serial killer? Were they stealthy? It seemed that a killer who entered women's bedrooms to kill and cover them with pillowcases would have to move like a cat.

"Just a skill I learned on the job. Why were you searching through my stuff?" His blue eyes drifted to the folder on the nightstand before focusing back on me.

I straightened hoping to gather some courage. "I called your reference, the landlord of your apartments. The number was for a Pet Mart."

He shrugged. "You must have dialed wrong, or maybe Trevor typed the wrong number. Now"—he reached for his towel—"You can stay here, pretending to look for my plate, but I'm going to get dressed. That means dropping this towel."

"No," I said sharply, a new blush creeping up my neck to my face. My reaction amused him. I wanted to kick myself and give him a little kick as well. "I'm leaving." I headed for the door in total humiliation and, at the same time, just as upset that I'd invited the entirely wrong person into my house.

I walked out and closed the door behind me. Cora was just coming out of her room. I decided not to tell anyone else about the Pillow Talk newspaper clippings.

I had no idea what prompted me, possibly just an ill-timed burst of optimism, but I stopped outside his door. Maybe we could still turn this whole thing around. Maybe I needed to give him a chance and not let my imagination run wild. I turned around and knocked on his door again.

He swung it open. Thankfully, he hadn't dropped the towel yet.

It took me a second to speak because of the whole muscular, naked chest thing. "Oh good, you're still decent."

A sly grin appeared. "I've been called a lot of things, but decent is not one of them."

I decided to ignore his latest attempt to shock me. I was convinced it was just a defense mechanism, something to keep people at arm's distance. It was time to counter his acerbic wit with some kindness. "There are no strangers here; just friends you haven't yet met. William Butler Yeats."

Those piercing blue eyes stared at me for a long moment. "A friend of the devil is a friend of mine. Tom Petty." He swung shut the door.

"He looks even better in a towel," Cora quipped behind me.

I spun around. "Oh shut up, Cora."

thirteen

I HADN'T REALIZED how badly I needed a diversion until I reached North Pond. Humiliation and worry did not make for a nice mix. The flurry of activity, food aromas and general excitement about the upcoming pirate battle helped take my mind off my troubles. For the next few hours, I was going to forget about Moon River and enjoy the festivities with my friends.

North Pond, a small lake situated at the base of Calico Peak afforded a lovely view of the northern lighthouse. The Old Man of the North, as we locals lovingly called it, was entirely different in architecture and size than his sister, the Southern Lady. The Old Man was erected in 1850, a saltbox style stone building with a small keeper's cottage and a brick red roof. The lantern was housed at the front peak of the building in a small black and white tower. A white picket fence surrounded it lending extra charm to its presence. But as sweet and cozy as it looked, it had an important job to do.

When a deep, unrelenting fog grabbed onto the island, the lantern spun with its big, golden eye, warning seafaring vessels to stay clear of the rocky shoreline.

While North Pond was a good distance from the actual coastline, the actors who'd set up camp around the pond had constructed half of a hull of a wooden pirate ship complete with a mermaid figurehead on the prow, billowing black sail and the British flag to let everyone know it was Captain Morgan's ship, the *Oxford*. Morgan, a privateer hired by the British navy, never flew a Jolly Roger like some of the other well-known pirates. There had been some heated discussion about creating a Jolly Roger with skull and crossbones for Morgan, only because it would have been more intriguing than the Union Jack, but that argument was shut down to uphold authenticity. The Hollywood caliber costumes were certainly flashy, but I doubted they were terribly authentic. Somehow, I visualized Morgan's crew as looking just a little more travel weary and grimy than the role players walking around in their crisp white shirts, green bandanas and red sashes. The Spanish soldiers were decked head to toe in quilted doublets and frilly collars. They donned silver helmets, the famous bonnet shaped conquistador helmets with the tipped up brim and the fin shaped blade that raced over the round top. Everyone looked impressive and ready for battle.

In the mid 1600s the infamous privateer Captain Henry Morgan, with his band of cutthroats and pirates, landed, ransacked and seized the Spanish town of Portobello in Central America. From the bits I'd read, the lucrative silver trade was motive for the attack. Morgan was successful and held the town ransom. It was considered quite the victory for Captain Morgan. So the ending of today's battle was not a mystery. Captain Morgan would be victorious.

Jack Drake, the owner of Pirate's Gold Restaurant, a swashbuckling themed eatery on the boardwalk, had hauled a barbecue to the site so he could sell some of his famous Cobs O Buttery Corn. He seasoned the delicious cobs with a mix of spices and parmesan. It was those fragrances that made me drift in the direction of his barbecue. Cora, Sera and her husband, Samuel, were already enjoying the grilled ears of corn. Opal had, after great debate, decided to skip the festivities to watch a Cary Grant marathon.

"Have you recovered from your interesting afternoon?" Cora asked. Sera avoided eye contact and worked hard at hiding a grin leading me to the conclusion that my sister had filled her in on the towel incident.

"I've recovered just fine," I said curtly.

"Hey, Anna, can I get you a corn?" Jack was a few years older than me (but younger than my sister who was now snickering behind her ear of corn). He'd been married once, but his wife grew tired of island life. Rather than follow her back to the mainland, Jack filed for divorce. His gray eyes looked pale in his suntanned, smiling face. He was sporting a black felt pirate captain's hat and jaunty neck scarf. Everyone, and by everyone I meant my sister, Sera and Opal, had tried to talk me into dating Jack. He was nice and charming and successful and he seemed anxious to give *us* a try, but I'd just never felt the spark, that spark I'd felt almost the second I met Michael.

"I will have one with the works, please." While I waited for my corn, Captain Morgan, the same Morgan I'd met at Molly's produce stand, climbed on a step stool with a megaphone to address the others. It was one of those quick gatherings before cameras rolled that a director might call on a movie set. I was fairly sure the real Morgan didn't need a megaphone. Barry Long, with his booming voice, didn't really need it either, but it was useful for getting everyone's attention.

Dozens of pirates and Spanish soldiers huddled around while Morgan read off a few instructions from a list he'd been handed. All the battle actors had impressive looking prop pistols and cutlasses at their sides. This was not a cheap, cheesy production. I was actually looking forward to the battle. It would certainly take my mind off things for awhile.

Cora, in her green Italian pantsuit, strolled up next to me. "I have to know—were you snooping around in his room?"

"Not exactly." I was a terrible liar. "Actually yes, exactly." The pirates and Spaniards were moving into place. "I don't want to talk about it. I'm out here trying to forget about it."

The entire walk to North Pond, I'd contemplated the different reasons Nathaniel might have for collecting articles about a serial killer. What if someone he knew, possibly even loved had been a victim? Was he on the island to forget about his terrible heartbreak? I'd considered that he was studying to be a journalist, and he was comparing writer styles as they all reported on the same subject. That one seemed a far stretch but not entirely out of the question. Even with all the scenarios I came up with, the one that kept creeping back was the theory that Nathaniel was the notorious Pillow Talk Killer. Something told me, serial killers liked to read about their murders. The one problem with that cold and chilling theory was that Nathaniel just didn't seem like a serial killer. He was aloof and, frankly, arrogant and there were more mysteries about the man than in a Nancy Drew book, but I just didn't get that serial killer kind of vibe from him.

Our modern day Morgan with his round belly and red and gold coat called everyone to their places. It was all quite organized and professional, but you could sense the edge of anticipation and excitement in the air. These actors were taking their roles very seriously. Hands hovered over weapons and gazes focused on opponents. A hush fell over the spectators gathered around the verdant green pastures, the makeshift battlefield. A whistle blew and action was called. I nibbled my flavorful corn, pushed the idea of serial killers and new tenants out of my head and got lost in the pirate fantasy unfolding in front of me.

fourteen

CORA and I both startled at the loudness of the prop guns. It was silly considering we were expecting the noise. Nevertheless, gunfire was always alarming, even when the weapons were shooting blanks. The sharp cracking sounds and the smoky smells reminded me of Fourth of July at the park with firecrackers and smoke bombs being lit to thrill the kids.

The entire reenactment event seemed to be going off without a hitch. The lush North Pond pasture was dotted with costumed characters. Even the *village folk* had their place in the melee. It started off quite choreographed, almost too organized and coordinated but, eventually, the actors loosened up and started having fun with it all. Captain Morgan, the easiest character to spot due to his size and flamboyant coat and hat, was focused on one of the Spanish soldiers. It seemed each actor was paired off with an opponent, and considering how the actual historical event concluded, it wasn't surprising to see a lot of the Spanish soldiers down on the grass in various dramatic poses of death.

Sera elbowed me lightly and leaned her head closer so I could hear her over the clamor. "Morgan is focused on that conquistador, the guy who held hands and sipped tea with two different women in the same morning." She laughed. "I hope he gets it good from ole Morgan."

Almost the instant she said it, Morgan aimed his pistol and fired. The man crumpled to the ground but with far less finesse than most of the other actors.

The ransacking of Portobello didn't take long, thankfully, and after a good twenty minutes of gunfire, yelling and very dramatic deaths, a victory was called and the pirates rejoiced. The day had started out crystal clear, but just like the morning after Fourth of July, a gray haze with the distinct aroma of gunpowder hung in the air. After a round of shoulder clapping and high-fives, a gesture I was certain was never used by the actual pirates, Morgan's crew walked over to the victims still curled, crumpled and folded on the grass and offered the corpses a hand up. Many didn't wait for hands up and started hopping to their feet. Cheers and applause thundered around the circle of spectators. Compliments about a job well done were being shouted across the field. There was general elation and celebration until Captain Morgan waved his hat in the air and whistled to get people's attention. He was standing over the still prostrate body of his victim, the two-timing Spanish soldier. The man wasn't moving.

Cora turned to me. "Do you think he fainted from all the excitement?"

I peered past the people starting to close in around the man on the ground. Concern dragged grave expressions around the circle like a solemn funeral procession. Barry Long wore the grimmest face of all. He held his hat to his chest and stooped down next to the man. He pushed off the man's helmet. Barry stumbled back and landed on his bottom. His face was as white as the linen shirt beneath his coat.

"Oh dear," Cora muttered as I raced past my friends and through the circle of spectators.

Barry looked up as I neared. "I think he's dead. He's been shot by a real bullet. Look at his head."

I knelt down next to the man. Beneath a bloody mat of hair, it was easy to spot a hole, a bullet hole, in his temple. I reached for his hand. It was limp and his arm felt like rubber. I searched for a pulse but couldn't find one. I wasn't surprised, considering a bullet through the temple left little chance for survival. We had a small medical clinic on the island, and there was one physician on call at all times. However, there wasn't anything a physician could do now except declare the man dead.

The elation and celebration had come to a cold, hard stop. People muttered to each other that he was really dead.

I looked over at Barry. "What was his name?"

"Was?" He turned a lighter shade, then swallowed hard. "My heavens. Arvin Meeks. I knew him professionally and socially. Nice man." He pulled his prop pistol out of the wide leather holster across his chest. "This is a cap gun. I couldn't have killed him," he insisted, though no one was accusing him. "I don't understand how this happened."

A few of the other actors finally worked up the courage to move closer. "What's happened?" a fellow conquistador asked tentatively. "Should we call an ambulance? Is Arvin all right?"

I stood up. "We'll need everyone to back up and clear the area." I found Sera's face in the crowd. She looked just as concerned and puzzled as everyone else. Most of the participants from the reenactment had gathered in small groups, talking quietly. Was there a killer amongst them? I had to assume that the bullet through the victim's head wasn't accidental, some terrible mistake with the props.

"Sera, could you and Samuel hurry back to the harbor and tell Frannie we need her to bring Detective Norwich over to the island. Tell him there's been a murder."

A gasp was followed by frantic conversations and people huddling closer. Sera and Samuel hurried off. I offered Barry a hand up but realized halfway through that I was not a great counterweight for someone Barry's size. I nearly fell forward. Somehow, between the two of us, we managed to get him to his feet and keep me on mine. As big as the man was and as impressive as he looked in his pirate garb, it seemed he needed to get to a chair and glass of water fast.

"Someone please get Barry to one of the tents. He needs to sit down. And bring him some water."

Barry had his big pirate hat in his hand, the gray ostrich feather had come loose and was dangling off the back of it as he trudged in his black boots toward the tents set up for costuming and refreshments.

Cora inched closer to me but preferred to stay far back from the body on the ground. She could not have looked more out of place in her pristine pantsuit and diamond watch. "Do you need me to do anything, Anna?" she asked from a good distance away.

"No, you can head home. Do you think Opal and you could manage dinner? I've got some cheese enchiladas in the freezer. You just have to defrost and heat." I hated the idea of leaving the others to fend for themselves with everyone so unsettled about the new houseguest, me especially, but it seemed I'd be stuck at the reenactment for awhile. At least until Norwich rudely shooed me away.

"I'm sure we can handle it. Does Opal know how to turn on the oven?" Cora asked.

"I'm pretty sure she does, and why don't you watch her while she does it so you too can learn some of the simpler tasks required of us regular folk."

"Well, you don't have to be so sarcastic." Morbid curiosity inched her a little closer but not too close. Her pointy heels on the grassy hillside weren't helping. She scrunched up her nose as if she could already smell death coming from the victim. "Is he really super dead?"

Only my sister would think there were varying degrees of death, just like there were varying degrees of wealth and beauty.

"He's super dead." A cloudy shadow fell over the hillside,

just in time to make the whole scene a touch more murder-y. "I think we might get showers later. You should get home."

She gasped as she looked down at her pantsuit. "I better. This outfit is dry clean only."

"All your clothes are dry clean only," I noted.

"Not those tacky sweats you bought me at Christmas."

"Forgive me for trying to add a bit of practicality to your wardrobe. Head on home, Cora, and try and stay clear of Nathaniel."

I shouldn't have said it because it instantly raised her curiosity. "Oh? Did you find something when you were snooping in his room? Aside from the obvious—"

"Which is?"

"Well, the man is built like a movie star."

I sighed partially out of frustration and partly because the day had finally pushed me over into the 'is it too early for bed' mode. "Go home, Cora."

"Right, as long as you're sure you don't need me."

I stared down at Arvin. One moment he was yelling, shouting and playing soldier, the next he was dead. I wasn't sure what my sister thought she might do to assist with her fancy clothes and her obvious aversion to dead bodies, but it was nice and out of character of her to ask. "I'm just going to wait for Detective Norwich."

"Isn't that that ornery policeman from across the channel, the one who is always chewing a toothpick and wiping his chin?" Cora asked.

"Inspector Clouseau," Jack quipped as he came up behind her. "Only, I like Norwich the Grinch better because he seems like a guy who would spoil Christmas." Jack marched rather stoically toward me, but as his gaze fell to the body on the ground, his confident steps faltered. He stopped a good fifteen feet away. No one liked to see a dead body. Ever since Barton Brown, a retired sheriff, left the island to live with his son in Boston, I'd somehow managed to fill the void when it came to crime on the island. I wasn't entirely sure how it started, but whenever someone wound up inexplicably dead, people said 'call Anna, she'll know what to do'. I kept reminding everyone that I had a degree in finance and not crime, but the locals had determined that lofty degree meant I should be put in charge in stressful situations. I'd felt fairly confident about my unanimously appointed role until this week when I'd made a reckless decision about my new boarder.

"Is there anything I can do?" Jack asked. His face was red from standing in front of the barbecue for so long.

"I'm afraid all I can do is wait for Norwich to arrive." I shook my head. "I think we can say this event has ended with a real bang."

fifteen

I HAD a good hour before Norwich arrived on the island. Most of the spectators had left the area. There wasn't much to see except a man lying crumpled and lifeless on the grass. It wasn't even a particularly gruesome death, enough to keep those more drawn to gore interested. The rest of the reenactment group had either gone to their tents or off to be away from the terrible reality of what had happened. I'd asked everyone to please stay on the island until the police arrived and warned them if they left it might raise suspicion. Naturally, I had no authority to keep them there, but I'd found a threat that fleeing might make them look guilty always worked.

I took photos of the victim from every angle to remember how and where he fell. Norwich, who disliked me and my *meddling* immensely tended to keep everything from me, so I used the time I had without his interference to gather some information.

On my way to the prop tent, I passed a woman who was crying and being comforted by two friends. She was no longer wearing the tavern wench costume, but I recognized the auburn hair and voluptuous lips. She was the woman I'd seen holding hands with Arvin over their cups of chai. She looked distraught enough that I decided to leave her alone for the time being.

A large tent, a fully enclosed model like one might see in the middle of a circus, had been erected for storing costumes and props. I'd been told a man named Alan Jessup was in charge of costumes and props.

A man, possibly in his thirties with thinning dark hair parted down the middle was seated at a small table. He was staring intently at the papers in front of him.

I walked farther into the tent. The outside breeze caused the tent to puff up and relax every few seconds, almost as if it were breathing. There were five rolling racks lined up along the canvas walls. The racks were filled with hangers, some empty, some heavy with costumes. Two large tables had been set with an array of boxes. Most were filled with various props, swords, pistols and even pewter tankards. The boxes were organized so that all the pistols were on one table and all the knives and cutlasses were on another. It seemed the pistols were all back in their boxes.

The man had been concentrating so heavily on his paperwork, he hadn't noticed me until I called his name. "Mr. Jessup?"

His face popped up. "Yes, oh, it's you. You're Anna. They told me you took charge out there. Are you with the police?"

"Not exactly." I stopped in front of his table. "In fact, not at all. It's just we don't have a police force on this island. We've sent for a detective from the mainland." I wasn't in the mood to explain more about the situation. A man was dead, and I was fairly confident the detective coming to investigate the case would either write it off as an accident or botch the case entirely, as Norwich was apt to do. It wasn't only because the man was inept at his job. He usually had crimes on the mainland that he considered far more important. As far as he was concerned, Frostfall Island was just a thorn in his side. He held the highly unpopular view that the island should be shut down and inhabitants forced to leave and all because of the occasional murder. Today's incident was certainly not the fault of the island locals. Most of the people in the reenactment did not actually live here. Including the somewhat frazzled man sitting in front of me.

"Have you gotten all the prop weapons back?" I asked.

He tapped a list in front of him. "I was just checking them all off. Everyone was anxious to rid themselves of their weapons." He stood and picked up the list. "Every prop, every costume has a number." We walked over to the boxes containing guns. "Do you see this number on the box? It corresponds with the number etched into the handle of the weapon. These are just cap guns. Apparently there were a few incidents with blanks, debris catching someone in the face or eye, so they spent the money on realistic cap guns."

"That's what I've heard. The pistol that Captain Morgan was holding," I started and saw that his eyes rounded immediately.

"Do you think Barry shot him?" Then he shook his head and answered his own question. "No, that would be jumping to conclusions. Barry was the first to turn in his weapon. He was shaken as can be. Never seen him like that. It was number six." He walked over and pulled a flintlock pistol from its box. Jessup admired the weapon for a moment, temporarily forgetting why we were looking at it. It was an impressive replica, a streamlined pistol carved out of dark walnut wood and adorned with engraved silver plating. "This is the gun I checked out to Barry." He waved his hand over the whole collection. "I've looked at them all. They might look impressive and menacing, but they are completely harmless."

"So someone must have brought a loaded gun to the reenactment. Did you know Arvin well?"

Jessup shrugged. "Not any better than the rest. I've only been working with this group for a year. It's just a part-time gig. I usually work for the university drama department. I don't participate in the role playing. I just keep things organized, write up schedules and help create game plans."

"Game plans?"

Jessup put the pistol back into the box. "Sort of like the schematic plans a football coach might draw up before a game."

My ears perked. "Then you probably have a drawing of where each actor was standing during the reenactment."

Jessup nodded and headed back to the table with all the papers. "That's what I was looking at when you walked in. It shows where each actor was standing when the starting whistle blew. Once the chaos begins, the more enthusiastic players tend to migrate from their assigned sections, but it does give a good idea of where everyone was on the battlefield."

"Would you mind if I took photos of your schematic game plan and your list of prop assignments?"

"Not at all. Especially if it will help." He turned the papers around on the table so I could take photos. "There were plenty of us taking pictures of the event, but once things got moving and smoke filled the air, the photo quality dipped fast. It's kind of creepy thinking someone out there is a killer."

I took several shots of the game plan and the lists. "Murder is always unsettling. You can't think of any reason someone would have wanted Mr. Meeks dead? Any arguments you might have witnessed, conflicts within the group?"

Jessup shook his head. "Like I said, I do this part-time. I try not to get involved in the group dynamics too much. I know there are conflicts and friendships and all that, but I stay out of it." Jessup's response seemed genuine. I had no reason not to believe him. He had easily allowed me access to some of the charts and lists that might be important in the investigation. It certainly would help to know exactly who was on the field and where they were standing.

"You've been a great help. I'd keep these papers handy. Detective Norwich will be arriving on the island soon. He may or may not ask to see them."

Jessup's brows bunched. "May or may not?" he asked.

"Yes, it all depends on whether he considers this case important enough to make the effort. It's one of the reasons I'm doing this. Frostfall Island falls under his jurisdiction, but we're always at the bottom of his priority list. Still, I think he'll want to see them. Can I leave my phone number, so I can get some photos from the event?"

"Uh yeah, I don't see why not." He handed me a slip of paper and found a pen.

I wrote down my number. "Thanks again. Do you happen to know where I might find Barry Long? I want to check in on him. See how he's doing."

"Last I saw him he was in the refreshment tent."

"I'll start there. Thanks again."

With so much going on at home, the last thing I expected or wanted was to be spending a long afternoon tracking down a killer, but it seemed, once again, I was wearing my investigator's hat and after this afternoon's horribly botched *investigation* at home, I wasn't feeling terribly confident. Even in my frazzled state of mind, I knew for certain that I'd do a far better job than the ignorant, arrogant man they were going to actually pay for the task.

sixteen

BARRY SEEMED GENUINELY SHAKEN after discovering that Arvin was dead, but that didn't take him off the suspect list. He had still been closest in proximity to the victim, close enough to manage to strike him right in a highly lethal spot, the left temple. The one thing that gave me pause about the Barry murderer theory was that of all the role players out on that lawn, Captain Morgan was the easiest to keep track of. There was no way to miss the large man wrapped in red and gold and shouting pirate curses. He was the center of the whole battle. Barry was a large, middle-aged man wearing big black boots and an unwieldy coat. He stood in the same spot while others raced, moved and turned about him. Never once did I see him move to the left flank of the Spanish soldiers. The only way he could have shot Arvin in the left temple was if Arvin had turned to the side. From what I saw, the soldiers and pirates moved toward each other head on, but I couldn't take anything off the table yet. It was too early in the case.

Barry was not in the refreshment tent. Most of the group had removed costumes, makeup and all hints of the reenactment. At least a dozen people were sitting at the long trestle tables eating fried chicken and mashed potatoes. The conversations were not loud and boisterous as one might expect after such an exhilarating event but then this day had ended tragically. That mood was evident in the tent.

Not wanting to interrupt their meal or get rumors started that Barry was the killer, I stopped short of asking if anyone had seen Mr. Long. Even without the red and gold coat, Barry Long was easy to spot. He stood a good head taller than the average person. Barry was standing in the shadow of the pirate ship talking on the phone. He hung up when he spotted me heading his direction.

I reached him. His thick gray hair was still wearing the outline of Captain Morgan's tricorn hat. He gazed up at the prow of the ship. "One minute, I'm Captain Morgan, the next I'm Barry Long and, I presume, a murder suspect."

I was slightly stunned by his comment. "You're not a suspect until evidence points your direction."

He pushed his phone into the pocket of his jeans. "Arvin Meeks was my target in the battle. I pointed my gun at him and fired."

"Yes, you pointed your prop flintlock at him, but that gun didn't kill Arvin Meeks. You need an actual bullet for that. I was just talking to Alan Jessup. He showed me the pistol you were using. It's about as lethal as a hairbrush. You could hit someone with it and it would probably leave a bruise, but it wouldn't rip a hole in someone's brain." I used the blunt terms to see what kind of reaction I got. It was just what I would have expected from someone who wasn't used to seeing dead people with bullet wounds. His ruddy complexion and sunburned cheeks looked ashen gray beneath the large shadow of the ship.

I moved a little closer. "Mr. Long, may I call you Barry? You can call me Anna."

"Yes, of course. I have a cousin named Anna," he said with a fond smile. "Growing up, I always sang Anna Banana when I saw her. She'd scrunch up her face all angry but that didn't stop me. She was fun to tease. What an ornery little devil I was. But I never hurt anyone," he threw that in briskly as if he'd suddenly considered that his childhood memory didn't put him in the best light.

"I used to hear the same taunt from kids at school, but I never minded too much. Barry, what can you tell me about Arvin Meeks? I'm trying to get a better picture of the victim."

Barry's thick fingers raked briefly through his hair. "He was in his early forties and not married. Grew up in New York and worked in Newport as a financial planner." Barry's mouth pulled tight, his lips sliding inwardly for a second before rolling back out. "Arvin was my financial planner." His face dropped. "This is going to sound like motive, but I'll just put it out there. It's all going to come out soon anyhow, once the police start investigating." I wasn't entirely sure about that, but I wasn't about to stop Barry as he divulged something important, something motive worthy.

"Arvin invested some of my retirement funds into a

company that turned out to be a scam. The president of the company, an investment firm, was a thief. Took off with all the funds, including a nice chunk of my retirement. Arvin didn't know the guy was a thief, but we were counting on him to do the research. Arvin was making a nice commission on the deal, so he looked past the gritty details, like the guy's shady history. But we're square on that. I'm not mad at Meeks for that anymore."

"Were there other people here who lost money through Meeks?"

"A few I think. I know Alan Jessup lost a chunk of change. I feel bad about that because I recommended Meeks to Jessup. In my defense, up until recently, Arvin had been giving me pretty solid advice. My retirement account was doing well."

"Alan Jessup, the prop manager?" I asked just to make sure. I was more than surprised to hear that he'd used Meeks as a financial adviser when he insisted he hardly knew the victim. "Were they well acquainted then? And Jessup took a financial hit too?" I seemed to be unraveling a good motive for Jessup, but the man was not on the field during the battle. Or was he? He had access to all the costumes. With the busy field and the battlefield chaos, it would have been easy to slip on a costume and get lost in the crowd.

"I wouldn't say they were well acquainted." We moved from under the shade of the boat as the afternoon sun disappeared for what looked like good. A layer of gray clouds had drifted in from the horizon. They'd brought with them the musty smell of rain and a sharp breeze. "Meeks did a lot of his consults over the phone. I was his client for five years, and we didn't meet face-to-face until he invited me to one of these reenactments. That's how I started up the hobby."

"But Jessup lost money too?" I didn't want to sound too anxious or start rumors, but I wasn't going to leave without the important details.

Barry sensed exactly where I was going with my questions. "Jessup seems like a real good guy." It wasn't an answer that matched my question, so I gave him a moment, hoping he'd fill in the rest. "He wasn't even out on the field." Captain Morgan had been busy sacking Portobello. He couldn't possibly have known if Jessup joined the battle in costume. "He lost some money but nothing too significant. After all, the guy is only in his thirties. He didn't have much to invest yet. He has time to make up the loss. Retirement is a long way off for him." Barry was certainly trying hard to layer on the reasons why it wasn't Jessup. I wondered if he was regretting sharing so much information. I was curious why it hadn't come up in my conversation with Jessup. I'd left the costume tent not even considering him a suspect, but now he was on the list.

I crossed my arms to shield against the cold wind now blowing across the field and adjacent meadow. A flock of redwing blackbirds had been twittering in the reeds along the bank of North Pond, letting everyone know they were back for the spring. The rippling water and sudden drop in temperature sent the birds to the shelter of some nearby black oak trees.

"Looks like it's going to rain," Barry said.

"And soon," I added. We turned to walk back toward the campsite and the warm, dry tents. Several of the group members had found an unused canvas tarp. They'd covered Arvin's body with it after I told them we needed to leave the body exactly where it was for the police.

My intent was to stay until Norwich arrived, but if he dawdled, which he was known to do, then I'd head off soon. I'd only face his scorn and ridicule anyhow, and I wasn't in the mood for either this afternoon.

A woman with vivid red hair was leaving the refreshment tent as Barry and I walked toward camp. She was huddled in a thick coat and cradling a cup of coffee in her hands.

Barry paused and lightly tapped my arm. "By the way, and this probably doesn't mean a thing but Arvin was a bit of a ladies' man. He never married and always considered himself a lifelong bachelor. Used to tell me there were far too many fish in the sea to settle for one catch. He hopped around a lot, but I know he was seeing two women in the group. Sarah Turner was the redhead you just saw hurrying across with her coffee cup. And Evie—"

"Auburn hair, sporty looking, trim and wearing a tavern wench's dress?" I asked.

He nodded. "Yes, that's her. You are a good investigator," he noted.

"That didn't take too much investigation. Arvin and Evie were having chai tea at my friend's tea house yesterday morning. They were quite cozy and stood out from the regular tea crowd because they were in full costume. That was how my friend, the shop owner, remembered that Arvin had been sipping tea with another woman, Sarah, just an hour before he sat at the table with Evie. Do you think they knew about each other?"

"Don't know how they couldn't? Gossip and rumors are pretty rampant in this group. Again, I don't know if it's important, but I thought you'd like to know. Though, it sounds like you beat me to it since you heard about his double tea time yesterday."

"This helps confirm it. Now I know some names just in case either woman had anything to do with Arvin's death. Motives of passion and jealousy are common." I was speaking freely and openly with the man about a murder that he might have committed. That told me my intuition had already written Barry off as the prime suspect. Unless he was putting Sarah and Evie into my path hoping to steer me away from him. That was always a possibility. I had to keep all avenues open.

In the distance, through the cold mist that was starting to shroud the island, a familiar, nasal voice, one that always made the hair stand up on the back of my neck, let me know my least favorite detective had arrived on the island.

I smiled faintly at Barry. "That will be the police. They'll take over and take care of Arvin's body. Thank you for all the information."

Barry nodded. "Are you going to fill in the detective?" he asked.

"If he asks. He prefers not to have my help. He'll probably

want to talk to you. Let him know everything you told me. It's all important at this point in the investigation."

The first drop of rain hit my forehead. I stared up at the dark, brooding sky. "Looks like it's going to be a good one. You should take cover." I waved to Barry and walked in the direction of the irritating voice.

seventeen

NORWICH ARRIVED in his puffy blue windbreaker, scarf and yellow rain hat as if he was just ferried out to some remote island in the middle of a hurricane rather than an inhabited island currently undergoing a spring storm, albeit it a cold, wet one. His investigative team consisted of one skinny officer, a young man with red rash where beard stubble should be. He looked anxious and a little excited to be at a murder scene. He also looked cold. Norwich had taken the time to bundle up like a kid going out to build a snowman, but he forgot to tell his assistant to bring a rain coat. His crisp uniform and the policeman's hat he tried so hard to keep on his head in the wind were soaked by the time they reached the camp. Norwich had an entire evidence team at his command, but he rarely brought them to the island. He considered it a waste of budget money and manpower.

Norwich was forty-something, but he wore it like sixty-something, with craggy lines in his forehead, floppy jowls and a beer belly that was always pushing the limits of his shirt buttons. The toothpick stuck out from the side of his mouth. It slid back and forth as he caught his breath after the walk from Island Drive. He kept a patrol car at the harbor, something he'd insisted upon after his first murder case on the island where he was offered a moped to get around.

Norwich rarely pulled the toothpick out of his mouth but always yanked it free from his slobbery lips when he wanted to scold me. "Well, well, well, if it isn't busy body St. James, the wannabe detective." His snide tone set my teeth on edge for just a second. It always took my body and mind a moment to absorb his awfulness. "Officer Peatman, if you see this woman anywhere near a crime scene, tell her to leave. She gets her nose into police business when she's supposed to be home sweeping floors and making biscuits for the crew of weirdoes living in her boarding house." His beady eyes turned back to Peatman. "Why didn't you bring a coat?"

The officer, on closer observation, was even younger and more anxious than I first thought. "Uh, sir, you didn't tell me where we were going just that you needed my assistance."

Norwich rolled his eyes as if that was a ridiculous excuse. He'd also had his fun with me, so he stuck the toothpick back between his lips. How badly I wanted to see him suck the pick straight back into his throat.

"What have you found out so far, St. James?" Norwich had the nerve to ask. He always showed up with a barrage of insults, then slyly tried to pry information out of me so he didn't have to do the legwork.

I placed a limp hand on my chest, batted my lashes at him

and turned on my Scarlett O'Hara voice. "Little ole me? How would I know anything about it? My brain is so filled with biscuit and cupcake recipes, I just don't have room for anything else."

The young officer chuckled, then quickly coughed, a clumsy attempt at covering it up.

Norwich's arrival was always my cue for a quick exit. With the heavy drizzle slowly plumping to large drops, I was just as happy to leave. Before we could exchange any more *niceties*, I headed toward Island Drive. Normally, Calico Trail would be a shorter, more scenic walk home, but the rain was sure to kick up a good deal of mud. It was hard to enjoy scenery in pouring rain. The paved road was my best bet.

"I better not find you're withholding information, St. James," Norwich called to my back.

He used the same threat every time, and every time, I ignored it. No matter what I told him, he was going to do a shoddy investigation, make a few rash decisions and make an arrest before looking at the evidence. His favorite saying was —'I want to close the books fast on this thing.' Only he never waited for the right ending before he snapped the cover shut.

Two men, still wearing the cotton shirts and padded doublets of the conquistador costumes, were carrying cups of coffee from the kiosk on the boardwalk. They hurried along with their heads ducked down to avoid the onslaught of rain. By the time I reached them as they stepped off Island Drive, the rain had slowed back down to a mist. It was my opportunity to ask a few of the other role players about the deadly battle scene.

One man looked to be in his thirties and wore the shirt and doublet well on his broad shouldered frame. Rain dripped from his wavy, blond hair. The second man was considerably shorter and stouter, compared to his friend. He had one of those permanently jolly faces with round cheeks and eyes sunk back deep in his face.

"Did the police arrive?" the taller man asked. He looked past me and squinted through the haze. "We heard people on the boardwalk say the police had arrived."

"Yes, Detective Norwich and his assistant are here. Judging by the doublets, I guess you two were fighting on the Spanish side this afternoon."

The shorter man nodded. "We sure were. Guess it could have been one of us."

"What do you mean?" I asked.

"Cameron seems to think Arvin just happened to step into the path of a real bullet," the taller one explained.

"C'mon, Deke." Cameron had to tilt his head back far to look at his friend. "Who would want to kill Arvin Meeks on purpose? He was a good guy."

"I don't know about that, Cam." Deke looked at me. He had a penetrating dark gaze, and it seemed he had something to tell me. I was all ears. "Supposedly, Arvin lost some people in the group a lot of money. He was some sort of financial planner, and he made a bad call on an investment."

My ears drooped back down. I'd been hoping for something new and sensational. Still, it was an important piece of evidence, and it seemed rumor had already gotten around to the rest of the group about Arvin's devastating misstep.

Obviously, Deke's mind had gone to that as possible motive. It seemed he wasn't on the same page as Cameron, who thought the whole thing was random and Arvin was in the wrong place at the wrong time.

"All I know," Cameron spoke up but then left a dramatic pause hanging in the air as he took a sip of coffee. The beverage was still hot enough and the air cold enough to push up a swirl of steam. It was quickly doused by the drizzle. "All I know," he repeated, "is that in the middle of all the craziness, noise and smoke, I saw Arvin drop out of the corner of my eye. At the time, I thought 'wow, that guy knows how to die'. It looked so real. Just *boom* like a sack of potatoes falling to the ground. Frankly, the rest of us take too long to die. There's the drama, the chest clutching, the moans and groans, the stumbling and faltering. I brought it up at our last meeting, but I was quickly shut down. Anyhow, I was thinking what a great, realistic job Arvin did. No theatrics. Just drop and die." Cameron was off on a bit of a tangent, and the rain was starting to get heavy again. His face dropped. His round cheeks made it hard for him to look sad but he managed. "I guess I know why it looked so real now." He shook his head. "Poor Arvin."

Deke squinted up at the sky. It was always such a normal, knee jerk reaction for people to look up at the clouds in a rainstorm, as if the clouds would have a little sign letting us know the duration and heaviness of the precipitation.

"Hey, Cam, we need to get these doublets and shirts back to Jessup before they're soaked," Deke said.

Cameron's eyes rounded. "You're right. Jessup is going to have our heads if we ruin these costumes."

"Sounds like you two are a little afraid of Jessup," I tossed the leading question out there to see if I could find out more about Jessup's character. I was still wondering why he never mentioned that Arvin had lost his money in the bad investment scheme.

"Nah, he's all right," Cameron said in an *aw shucks* kind of tone. "He just takes his job really seriously."

"Well, you two better hurry. Stay dry," I called as we parted.

By the time I reached Island Drive, rain was pelting me from every direction. I ducked my head, crossed my arms around me and picked up my pace. Not that any of that would help. I was going to be drenched by the time I got home.

eighteen

A HOT SHOWER and change of clothes erased the chills I'd developed on my walk home. Cora had taken the cheese enchiladas out of the freezer, but it seemed she'd left the hard part, turning on the oven and placing the tray into that same heated oven, to me. She'd texted halfway through my walk back that she was exhausted from pirates and murder and all that and needed to take a nap before dinner. That was my clue that dinner wasn't going to be close to ready on time.

    I hurried down the hallway to get things going in the kitchen. I could hear Cary Grant's distinctive voice coming through Opal's door as I walked past. At the other end of the hallway, Nathaniel's door was shut, but light was seeping out from the bottom. I wondered if my intrusion into his personal belongings would push him to leave the house. I wasn't sure how I felt on that prospect. As much as it would erase some of the uneasiness in the house, it also meant that

I'd have to start the search all over again. I wasn't guaranteed the next person would fit well either. We were a unique lot, a square hole and it seemed the world was filled with round pegs. Although, I wasn't sure I'd call Nathaniel a round peg. He was more that odd star shaped peg that only fit into the hole one way.

I stopped by the small alcove on the bottom floor where I kept a computer and printer for everyone's use. I downloaded the photos of Arvin's body, along with the schedules and lists from Jessup's desk. I'd exited the costume tent, Jessup's tent, without even a hint that he was the killer, but by the time I left the grounds, I'd added Jessup back to the list. Sometimes withholding information was more damming than laying it all out in the open. If he'd admitted to me right away that he'd been caught up in Arvin's sketchy investment scheme, I probably wouldn't have thought any more about him as a suspect. But since he left it out of our conversation entirely, even after I asked how well he knew Arvin, that seemed like a red flag.

I plucked the photos off the printer and walked to the broom closet. I leaned in and pulled out the two corkboards. The red and blue pushpins sat just where I'd left them waiting to hold important information and photos about the Meeks case. "I can't believe there's been another murder," I said to no one, but the corkboards seemed to agree. I pulled the boards out whenever I had a new case, and it seemed I was doing it more often than not.

I carried my supplies to the kitchen and hung the cork boards from the hooks on the one clear wall in the kitchen.

At one time they held some whimsical rooster photos and a small chalkboard where we'd leave messages for each other like 'will be late for dinner' and 'we're out of milk'. But as I was thrust more and more into the role of island investigator, I realized the corkboards needed a prominent place to hang. So the message board came down, which was fine. Texting was easier, more permanent and less messy than chalk.

"The oven," I reminded myself and hurried over to turn it on. Dinner was definitely going to be later than usual. It seemed both Tobias and Winston had been delayed by the rain so that worked. With the oven set, I returned to the boards. Let's see Norwich solve the crime all while fixing dinner for six, I thought wryly.

Not long ago, the man's rude comments and condescending attitude would really set my hair on fire, but once I started solving cases, leaving him mostly in the proverbial dust, I stopped fretting about his comments. He was a jealous, angry, inept man who didn't deserve my time.

Some people might have thought it a little cringey to post photos of a body near the kitchen table. In fact, not *some* people but most people. The Moon River bunch didn't mind at all. They enjoyed watching the evidence unfold. While they preferred that I did most of the legwork, they loved being part of solving the puzzle. Since the new tenant took his meals in his room, I didn't have to worry about offending him at the dinner table with photos of Arvin Meeks, pale and lifeless with a hole in the side of his head.

That thought took me right back to earlier in the day when I'd discovered many articles about the Pillow Talk Killer on Nathaniel's bedside table. Was that what he preferred for reading material? Gory descriptions of murder and mayhem by an elusive monster, a monster with a sugary sweet romantic side. Or was there a more sinister reason for him to be collecting the articles?

I pushed the worrying thought from my head. I was jumping to conclusions. I'd already jumped, too far it seemed. I'd never done anything as rude as search a tenant's room. I was ashamed of what I'd done. At the same time, I felt a sense of urgency in learning all about Nathaniel Smith. That triggered something else. I pulled out my phone and scrolled to the number I'd called to talk to his landlord. I looked at the phone and at the number on the email. They were the same. I hadn't misdialed. Had the landlord typed the wrong number? I'd done it more than once myself.

I put my phone down on the desk and headed back to the corkboards. I hung the four photos of the body showing where he'd landed in relation to the surrounding campsite. One showed a close-up of the bullet hole. It really had been a clean shot according to my unprofessional estimates. That was one disadvantage I had in my investigations, a lack of forensic and autopsy reports. I had one friend at the mainland precinct, the station where Norwich kept his office. I envisioned a sloppy office with paperwork everywhere and empty coffee cups filled with dried creamer and discarded toothpicks. The usual family photos would be lacking because the man had no family. My friend, Mindy, used to live on the island and moved back to the mainland when she got married. She worked in the files office at the precinct.

Occasionally, something would pass her desk about a Frostfall Island case, and she'd share the information with me. Otherwise, I was on my own. Well, not entirely on my own since my Moon River family would help me sort out evidence and create a theory or two. That reminded me that I planned to cook some chocolate pudding for dessert. It wasn't the perfect accompaniment for cheesy enchiladas, but Tobias had been asking for it. Since he had been quite out of sorts about the new boarder, I thought a nice bowl of pudding with whipped cream might soothe his nerves.

I pulled out the milk, cocoa and sugar and set it near the stove, then returned to the corkboards to pin up the rest of the photos. The schematic drawing of where the role players stood during the battle would be the greatest help of all. As long as people stayed in the sections they were assigned, I could highlight the names of the people who were positioned to the left of the victim. I pinned the photo of the schedule and the prop list to the board and stood back. It was just the beginning of a case, but I had a good start.

The oven pinged letting me know it was ready. I pushed the tray of enchiladas into the oven, grabbed my apron and set to work on the pudding. I took some eggs out of the basket and broke them into a bowl. I was whisking in corn starch, concentrating on my task when a deep voice startled me.

"And you were worried about me," Nathaniel said sarcastically.

I spun around so fast, I sprayed egg yolk around the kitchen. It took me a second to catch my breath. Nathaniel was standing at the corkboards staring at the dead body photos.

"Sorry, didn't mean to scare you," he said. "I guess I'm doing that a lot." He was wearing a black sweater. Annoyingly, all I could think about was that naked chest and the scar. Was it a bullet hole or was that me jumping to conclusions again?

"No, you didn't scare me—well, yes you did. I was concentrating on my pudding and—" I took another short breath. "How on earth do you manage to move without making any sound?"

His smile was never disappointing. "Honestly, I think I learned the skill as a teenager. I got grounded a lot, and to avoid being stuck in my room for my entire teens, I taught myself to sneak past the living room unnoticed. My parents were always watching television, so I managed to go out and see my friends."

"Even when you were supposed to be grounded."

He shrugged. "Then I'd usually get grounded for sneaking out. It was sort of an ugly cycle. You get the picture. And speaking of pictures—" He tapped the one that clearly showed a bullet through Arvin's temple. "Interesting hobby you've got."

"I hope it's not too disturbing for you."

A small, light chuckle followed. Not the response I was expecting. Why was it not disturbing? Was he used to seeing dead people?

I walked over to the corkboards. "There was a pirate reenactment on the island this afternoon. This man was playing the part of a conquistador. There was a big battle, fake of course, only it was far too real for Arvin Meeks. He's dead."

"Shot in the temple," Nathaniel noted.

"Exactly. Do you know much about murder?" The clumsy question fell from my lips before I could stop it.

Another chuckle. At least he wasn't still sore about my earlier invasion of privacy. At the same time, he seemed to find murder an amusing subject. "I try to stay away from murder if that's what you're asking. Why all the photos? Are you part of the island police? Is that why you thought you could snoop through my stuff?" Maybe he was still a little sore.

"Unfortunately, there is no island police," I said, again before I could stop myself. If the handsome man standing in my kitchen was the Pillow Talk Killer, then I'd just given him the green light to kill because he knew there was no one around to arrest him.

His deep blue eyes narrowed. "So, they put the boarding house owner in charge of murders?"

"Not exactly. I'm the person everyone counts on to solve crimes. It's a long story. When there is a serious crime, we call Detective Buckston Norwich to the island. He's at the site now but he's—" I trailed off, deciding I'd divulged enough about the lack of security and police presence on the island.

"Let me guess—Norwich is a sloppy dresser, always has a spot of mustard on his tie, and he thinks investigating murders on this island is beneath him or a waste of time so he rushes haphazardly through the evidence and interviews and ends up with the wrong person or empty-handed."

Nathaniel waited with a slight grin for me to confirm or deny his *guess*. Only, I was so flabbergasted by how spot on he was with Norwich's description, I was speechless. The only thing he missed was the toothpick.

"Well?" he prodded.

I shook my head lightly to restart my brain. "It's almost as if you know the guy. Do you?"

He shrugged. "I figured if the island is counting on the owner of the boarding house to solve murders, then the local detective must be a fumbling idiot." He surveyed the photos once more. "Does it happen a lot?"

I was still somewhat stunned by our conversation and wasn't following his line of thought. "Does what happen a lot?"

"Murder. It's such a small island. It seems so peaceful."

"And far away from civilization," I said pointedly, using his own words. I sighed. "I would say—if using statistics—I mean if we were to look at population size and average—you know—murders, then it could be mathematically stated that Frostfall Island has more murders than it should."

A short laugh shot from his mouth. "I don't know if that was sugarcoating or just a tangled, elaborate way to say yes, Frostfall Island has a lot of murders."

I felt my cheeks warm. "I suppose your way of putting it would have been a bit more to the point. Opal thinks the place is cursed."

His eyes were cobalt blue under the kitchen lights. They reminded me of a porcelain vase my grandmother kept in her curio cabinet.

"I think we're making progress," he said.

"Sorry?" I wasn't following again. This time it might have been the blue eyes.

"You didn't follow up that statement about the island being cursed with an open invitation for me to leave. Seems like it would have been a good opportunity."

"I guess I have been jumping at those opportunities. I'm sorry. If you're satisfied with the accommodations—"

"I am and the food is good." He tilted his head side to side. "Lacking in bacon and burgers but it'll be good for my health."

I nodded. "Right. Well, speaking of food, I've got to get back to my stove. I'm cooking chocolate pudding for Tobias. He's been a little out of sorts…" I stopped, realizing I couldn't finish the sentence.

"That would be because of me. I can be a little brusque," he admitted.

"A little."

"I'll try and work on it. In the meantime—" Once again those penetrating blue eyes, only this time with a wry arch of his brow.

My cheeks warmed again. "I promise I won't snoop in your room."

"Thanks. Looking forward to the pudding," he said as he walked out of the kitchen.

Maybe that shoe pebble had finally slipped to a more comfortable place permanently. Now I just had to convince the others of it.

nineteen

NORMALLY, on an evening after a murder on the island, the entire conversation would be about the case. But tonight, as the sun set outside the kitchen window and a cool mist settled over the island, the Moon River tenants were hunched over their dishes of whipped cream topped puddings murmuring about the new boarder.

After our chat, I'd hoped that Nathaniel would consider eating his cheese enchiladas or pudding with the rest of us, but the extra chair sat empty. It gave the others a chance to air their suspicions and grievances, and they had plenty. Mostly, they'd all landed on one particular theory that had them all rushing through their pudding, a dessert that was normally savored.

Opal plowed a big chocolatey bite into her mouth and just as quickly swallowed. "I'm just saying it's an awfully big coincidence."

I sat down with a cup of hot tea. I'd done enough taste

testing of the pudding that I needed to skip a bowlful or risk going into pudding overload. "What coincidence?" I asked.

Tobias scooted forward on his chair. He had a whipped cream moustache, but none of us would embarrass him by letting him know. Normally, he kept out of gossip and he was always an avid napkin user, but he was keenly interested in the topic, so interested he'd skipped his usual napkin wipe. "Well, Anna, it doesn't take an accountant to put two and two together." He paused to smile about his pun, then took a moment to wipe his face. Everyone around the table sighed silently in relief. (It was hard to keep a straight face when talking to someone with a whipped cream moustache.)

"What two and two?" I asked.

Cora moaned in irritation. "Oh please, Annie." Cora was the only person on this earth who could get away with calling me Annie, and she used it whenever she was annoyed with me. She held up one palm. "Arrival of one Mr. Smith." She held up the other palm. "Murder on Frostfall Island." She clapped her hands together. "Get the picture?"

I blinked at her over my cup of tea. "You're just angry because he didn't kiss your hand."

"Am not. Even though, I must admit, and begrudgingly so, the man looks fabulous in a towel—"

That statement pulled everyone's focus to my sister. Opal's mouth dropped. "Did you see Gable and Gardner's love child in a towel?"

Cora smiled, thrilled to have everyone's complete attention. "Yes, and he did not disappoint. Anna can confirm."

All eyes turned my direction, with the exception of

Winston. This turn in conversation was making him uncomfortable. I had to agree.

"Anyhow," I said with a huff of air. "I was at the event, and I never saw Mr. Smith. Also, the gun was shot at close range. Mr. Smith was not on the field during the battle."

Opal wiped her mouth. After the whipped cream moustache incident, it seemed everyone was using their napkin more than usual. "I have to agree with Anna. It couldn't have been Mr. Smith."

Cora and Tobias glared at her as if she was a traitor.

"And that is based on what?" Tobias asked sharply. The poor man desperately wanted to see our new housemate walking out the door with his bags.

Opal pushed the sleeves of her silk housecoat up on her arms. "Because I heard music coming from his room when I took a break from the Cary Grant marathon. It was right between 'To Catch a Thief' and 'His Girl Friday'. I'd sipped down three iced teas in a row, so the little girls' room called. An old rock song.—" she tapped her chin and her eyes rolled up. "The Eagles, I think." The satiny sleeves slid down again as Opal sat back sure that she'd solidified Nathaniel's alibi.

Tobias wasn't about to take it as solid. "How on earth does that clear the man?"

Opal's mouth puckered as if she'd sucked on a lemon. "Because my break was at the same time the pirate escapade was taking place at North Pond. Unless Mr. Smith knows how to be in two places at once, he could not have been at the reenactment."

Tobias put down his spoon rather loudly. His bowl had

been nearly licked clean of pudding. I'd hoped having his favorite dessert would wipe away some of the bitterness he was feeling about the new arrival. Clearly, that was not the case.

"How do you know he was inside the room? Did you actually see him?"

Winston cleared his throat. "Um, our voices are getting kind of loud."

I winked at him. "Winston is right. Tobias, I know there's some chafed feelings between you and Mr. Smith—Nate—but I think we should avoid jumping to conclusions. I was at the murder scene, and there was no sign of him. In addition, I have posted the names of the people who were on the field during the reenactment. I was witness to the whole thing. Naturally, as people were dying from the pretend battle, I had no idea there was an actual casualty until the field cleared. As you can see, the corkboards are up, and I've got some information to share. Let's drop the current subject and focus on the case. Norwich arrived on the island—"

Just saying his name produced a series of dry laughs, scoffing sounds and eye rolls.

"Exactly," I said. "You all know what that means. We're going to need to find out who killed the conquistador. Was it friend or foe, pirate or Spaniard? Someone out on that field shot Mr. Meeks dead with one bullet. Let's find the killer."

twenty

IT WAS a spring evening but the chill in the air prompted calls for some cocoa. Apparently, the homemade double-chocolate pudding in which I'd added chunks of bittersweet chocolate along with the cocoa powder had not been enough of a chocolate fix. I was putting away the extra whipped cream when Opal suggested it would be nice on top of cocoa. Everyone had immediately agreed. Everyone except my sister, that is. Cora had decided that she'd had enough murder and mayhem for one day and flounced off to her bedroom. Winston was on the fence about the cocoa until the rich, velvety aroma circled the kitchen, prompting him to sign on for half a cup.

Opal and Tobias cradled their hands around their mugs while Winston set to work stirring his whipped cream into the cocoa to cool it.

I stood at the corkboards, like a teacher waiting to have

the attention of her students. "If you're all settled in with your cocoa, I'd like to create a chart of possible killers."

Tobias wiped his mouth and sat forward. "Right. What do you have so far? How do we narrow the field, so to speak?" He chuckled. (It seemed the double chocolate night had lifted his spirits after all.) "I suppose it's not just metaphorical. We are actually going to narrow down the field." He raised his brows. "That was the way you were heading, right?"

"Exactly. You get a gold star for the day."

Opal scoffed. "If I knew you were giving out stars—" She waved her hand. Her kimono style sleeves, the ones she'd attempted to push up all night, fluttered in the cool kitchen air. "That's right. I've already got my star on the Walk of Fame. Carry on, Anna."

"Thank you." I was thankful she didn't go into a long narrative about how she missed the star ceremony because she was long dead when they finally started the Hollywood stars. She'd lamented that misfortune more than once. The funny thing was she talked about going to Hollywood to see the star in person but had never made it there. She claimed that the west coast held too many sad memories from her days as Valentino, culminating with his unfortunate death.

Winston stopped the conversation with a loud slurp. He looked up over the rim of his mug and smiled. "Oops." He lowered the mug. "I was trying to get that little lump of chocolate out of the bottom. But I think that last moment of humiliation is my cue to head to bed. We got in three orphaned baby raccoons, and we've already named them the three stooges. They are comics. They're also a handful." He stood up to put his mug in the sink. "Good luck with the murder."

"The cast members are slowly peeling away from the set," Opal said. I was sure that her exit would follow. She never had much patience for case solving, but it seemed she was staying.

My class had shrunk but with cocoa mugs drained, it seemed I had their full attention. Using two push pins, I hung up a blank sheet of paper. I uncapped my marker. "Here is where the fake pirate ship sat overlooking North Pond."

"There was even a pirate ship," Opal said. "Wow, this whole thing was quite elaborate."

"Quite," Tobias noted. "There were swashbucklers and conquistadors strolling along the boardwalk and past my office all morning. It was quite the sight to see and different from my usual view of the museum parking lot. Where was the victim standing?" Tobias asked.

"I was just getting to that." Even though I considered myself a fair artist, for brevity sake I tended to use stick figures on my case charts. I did add a pirate's hat on my Captain Morgan stick figure. No need to go entirely uninspiring on the diagram. "I've placed an X for where Meeks stood according to the chart. This is where Barry Long, Captain Morgan, stood, just fifty feet or so from his ship. I mention Barry because his character, Morgan, was slated to shoot our victim, Arvin Meeks. I witnessed him aim his flintlock at Arvin, but the pistol he held was a cap gun, no more lethal than a feather duster."

"Interesting." Tobias rubbed his chin with his thumb and forefinger. "So the man who was supposed to kill Meeks in the choreographed battle shot his intended victim and rather than die a theatrical death, the man actually died. It sure seems like he should be a suspect."

I pointed my marker at Tobias. "Yes, that makes sense and on top of that, Barry had motive. It seems that Arvin Meeks, a financial planner, recently made a very bad investment with some retirement funds. Barry was one of his clients. Which brings me to a second victim of the financial scam, Alan Jessup." I added a few triangles and wrote costume and prop tent across the figures. "Jessup was also harmed by Meeks' poor investment advice. He is in charge of costumes and props. However, he is not on the schematic drawing for the battle."

"But if he was in charge of costumes," Opal said. "He could have slipped one on and snuck onto the field."

I nodded. "And with the chaos surrounding the reenactment and battle, no one would have noticed." I placed a stick figure to the left of the X and wrote the name A. Jessup beneath it with the notation that he was not one of the role players. I looked at the added comment. "Of course, this makes it possible for just about anyone to have snuck onto the field. Maybe the chart isn't going to help."

"Nonsense," Opal said. "The costumers take their jobs very seriously. I highly doubt Jessup would have lent out a costume if it wasn't on his list. However, it would be easy for him to take a costume if he was in charge. But he wouldn't have let just anybody take off with one of those outfits."

I nodded. "Good point. We'll leave Jessup here, but I'll add a question mark to remind us that he was not technically supposed to be on the field."

"If he was shot in the left temple, then the assailant had to be standing to the left of the victim," Tobias said eagerly. Considering the only holiday that ever got the man excited was tax day, it was quite the show of enthusiasm.

"Exactly right. According to the chart Jessup gave me, Arvin might have died from friendly fire."

Opal scratched her forehead. "You've lost me. How could a friend have shot Arvin? Was it just an accident?"

"No, by friendly fire, Anna is referring to the different sides of the reenactment, the battle between pirates and Spaniards. She's saying that someone dressed as a Spanish soldier shot Arvin. They were supposed to be fighting on the same side. That's why it's called friendly fire. It's generally considered a terrible, tragic accident when it comes to real war, but in this case, there were no real enemies. Only actors in costumes." Tobias sat back with a satisfied grin. It seemed the double chocolate pudding followed with a hot cocoa had given him a burst of energy. He was rarely so talkative. I was pleased that his interest in the new case had taken his mind off the new tenant. Unfortunately, his long-winded explanation had lost Opal entirely.

Her round shoulders lifted and fell. "Now that I'm more confused than ever, I'm heading off to bed. Friday night is Jimmy Stewart night on the late night movie channel. Ciao, arrivederci, and good night."

With a flounce, followed by watery silk and long flowing sleeves, Opal left the kitchen.

Tobias stifled a yawn. "Who do we have on the left side of Meeks on the plan?"

"You sure you want to keep going?"

"Absolutely."

"Wonderful. So according to the names on the plan, we have a man named Deke Silverton. He stood here." I put another stick figure to the left of Arvin's X. I wrote the name down, then snapped my fingers.

Tobias sat up straighter. "Do we have our man?" There was a little disappointment in his tone. It was always nice to solve a crime, but if it came too fast it was like finishing a chocolate chip cookie too fast, yummy but far less satisfying.

"No, but I think I met Deke. He and another man in Spaniard doublets were coming back from the coffee kiosk. Deke brought up the issue of Arvin making bad investments for people in the group. Otherwise, I have nothing else connecting him to the crime except he was standing in a good spot to shoot Arvin in the left temple." I returned to the chart. "Now here's something interesting. Evie Stern was dressed as one of the villagers, a tavern wench to be exact. She was one of the actors standing within the battlefield to make it look more spontaneous. After all, Morgan ransacked the town, so it made sense they mixed villagers into the crowd. Evie's location was to the left of the victim."

"Do you think she might have killed him?" Tobias asked, stifling yet another yawn. The burst of chocolate energy was being zapped by a long day of working with numbers.

"She had motive, though slim at best. It seems aside from being an untrustworthy financial advisor, our victim was also not dependable when it came to romance. He was seeing not one but two women from the group. One of them was Evie, the tavern wench."

Tobias lifted his napkin to hide his third yawn. I snapped the cap back onto my pen. "And third time is a charm, so head up to bed, Tobias. We can revisit this tomorrow. Thanks for your help."

Tobias didn't bother to argue. His lids were looking heavier by the second. (Chocolate overload probably helped with that.) He carried his cocoa cup to the sink. "Good night, Anna."

"Good night, Tobias. And, Tobias"—I stopped him just before he walked out. His sleepy eyes turned back to me —"Try not to worry. I'll make sure everything straightens itself out."

He nodded quietly and left the room.

twenty-one

IT SEEMED I was in for another restless night. Midnight had fallen over the island and all was quiet except my thoughts. They were as noisy, active and jumpy as a bunch of toddlers in a bounce house. By the time I'd stopped theorizing about this afternoon's murder, another more relevant topic popped up—Nathaniel Smith. After the utter embarrassment of being caught snooping in his room, I'd tried to wash the whole event from my head. But those articles about the Pillow Talk Killer kept poking at me. Why had Nathaniel collected them?

Huck grumbled at the end of the bed. He lifted his big head and sneered at me for waking him as I climbed out from under the covers. I didn't bother with slippers as I plodded across the room to my dresser where I'd left my laptop. I picked it up and with much colder feet than when I'd left the bed, I hurried back to the warmth of the covers. It was still early enough in spring that midnight meant frosty dew and chilly temperatures. Summer couldn't come soon enough.

I climbed back in and once again disturbed Huck's sleep by shoving my feet underneath the quilt and beneath him. "Sorry, buddy," I said as he lifted his large head again. "You're the best thing for cold feet." I flipped open the laptop. It took me a moment to adjust to the glowing light, then I typed in Pillow Talk Killer. Not surprisingly, there were millions of results.

I clicked open an article from the *Newport Times*. It was dated six months earlier, the last time the monstrous serial killer claimed a new victim. "The notorious Pillow Talk Killer has struck again," the article started. "Twenty-nine-year-old Rhonda Myers was killed in her home. A large heart and XO were drawn on the victim's bathroom mirror in red lipstick. Myers was stabbed multiple times. Her head had been covered with a pillowcase. Police confirmed that the latest horrible murder was most assuredly the work of the Pillow Talk Killer, a serial killer who has taken eight lives, all women, in the past six years. The PTK attacks are sporadic and spaced far apart making it even harder to catch the maniac. There was no sign of forced entry, also a hallmark of the PTK. That has led authorities to develop several theories. One is nicknamed the cat theory, which purports that each of the victims had one thing in common; each of them had left their front door or windows unlocked, and the killer, quiet and stealthy as a cat, was able to enter the house and bedroom without being heard. The second theory, a more sinister one, if possible, is that the killer knew his victims, perhaps even charmed his way into their lives and bedrooms. Both theories and the repetitive evidence have not led to an arrest, leaving law enforcement frustrated and embarrassed."

I clicked open the next article and instantly shut it. Somehow, a photo of a victim had been posted, and it was gruesome. (And that coming from someone who had seen more than her share of dead bodies.)

The photo of the bloodied victim had left my heart pounding. It was more brutal than most of the victims I'd come across in my investigations. I shut the laptop, and the room was instantly drowned in darkness. My research session was only going to add to the restless night.

A breeze outside pushed the branch of the backyard red maple against my window. It was a sound I'd heard a million times, every time a wind blew up from the coast, but the frightening vision of a serial killer, the PTK, climbing through an open bedroom window sent me down deep into my covers.

Huck had had enough of my restlessness. With a doggish grunt he rose to his big feet and dropped down to the carpet next to the bed. The room was dark, but I caught his look of disdain just before he rested his big head down. That same head popped right back up, fully alert with ears pointed in the direction of the hallway. I'd heard the noise too, only it seemed to be coming from downstairs.

A low thump caused me to sit up, only, embarrassingly, I realized it was just my pulse pounding in my ears.

I was the owner of the boarding house, I reminded

myself. If my tenants were in danger, I needed to take charge. I had to tell myself that a few times before I found the courage to lower my feet to my slippers. I grabbed my fuzzy green robe and pulled it on, hastily tying the belt around my waist before opening the door. Huck, the brave watchdog, huddled behind me, leaning his head past my legs to get a look at the hallway.

"Glad you have my back, Huck," I whispered with an eye roll.

I stepped into the hallway. All seemed as it should, the glow of the nightlights helped point the way to the bathrooms and the stairway on a dark night like tonight.

The smallest of sounds came from downstairs. I stared down to the bottom landing and grabbed hold of the banister. It took a few seconds to will my feet forward. On my slow, cautious descent I asked myself why I hadn't carried something with me, like a fire poker or the tennis racket in my closet. It wasn't as if I'd actually played a game of tennis in years. It could have been put to good use here. Instead, it stayed new and pristine in my closet.

I was halfway down the stairs when Huck, the cowardly lion, raced past me down to the landing. He headed straight to the kitchen. I wasn't sure if he thought I'd decided to get up in the middle of the night to give him a treat or if he hurried ahead to greet someone. It was the latter.

Nathaniel sat alone in the dark at the kitchen table eating the last bit of pudding. Again, something grabbed at my chest. Even though my dog sat like a sentry at his side, he looked lonely, lost, a man looking for something that he just couldn't find.

"I couldn't sleep," he confessed. "Then I shamelessly came down here hoping to find more pudding." He lifted the half-empty bowl. "Were you coming down for the same reason? You can have the rest. It's the best pudding I've ever eaten. My grandmother used to make pudding like this on Christmas Eve. She'd top it with broken crumbs of candy canes."

I sat at the table just around the corner from where he sat. "I couldn't sleep either, but you may finish the pudding. I'm glad it reminds you of your grandmother. Why couldn't you sleep? Let me know if you need more blankets or another pillow."

His thick hair was sticking out in every direction as if, like me, he had tossed and turned before giving up any hope of sleep.

"The room and bed are perfect. Just had stuff on my mind." He dug his spoon into the bowl.

I smiled. "Like my chocolate pudding?"

"This pudding was definitely on the list. How about you? What was keeping you awake?" He motioned toward the corkboards on the wall. "Murder?" There was just enough of a teasing quality in his tone to assure me he wasn't only talking about the Meeks case.

"I'm just looking out for the people in this house. They've put their trust in me and—"

"Anna—" His deep voice was as rich and smooth as the

pudding in front of him. "Your band of merry misfits is safe. Like I said, I'm just here to—"

"Get away from civilization," I finished for him.

His dark lashes dropped for a second, then that deep blue gaze returned. "Yes." He picked up his spoon again. "Saw a photo on the mantel in the front room. Is that Mr. St. James?"

"My father?" I asked, then realized he was talking about the photo of Michael and me standing in front of the southern lighthouse. "My maiden name is St. James. I kept it after I married Michael. His name was Stratton."

"Was?" He finished the last bite of pudding and gently placed the spoon down. "I'm sorry. I don't mean to pry."

"No, that's all right." I had no idea why but the way Nathaniel looked at me, in the shadowy light of the kitchen, made me start spilling the story. "Michael was a fisherman. I left a job in finance on the mainland to become a fisherman's wife on Frostfall Island. A year after we said our nuptials, Michael sailed off on his trawler and never returned. His boat was found on a reef, broken and battered and empty. No sign of Michael. A year ago, on the eighth anniversary of his disappearance, he was declared officially dead. Divorce is hard. Widowhood is hard, but I can tell you from experience that being stuck between those two realities is even worse. I only wish I had more closure, some kind of proof that he's truly gone."

He stared at me for a long moment. It seemed the kitchen and the entire house fell away, and it was just the two of us sitting in a meadow in the middle of nowhere. "I'm sorry about that," he said, cracking that odd vision I had of the two of us alone in the world. "Sounds rough."

I swallowed back the ache that always returned when I talked about Michael. As often as I thought of him, I rarely spoke about him aloud. But something had prompted me this evening. I was blaming it on being tired. Nothing was ever normal or easy to understand once the clock passed midnight.

"What about Mrs. Smith?" I asked. "Not your mother but a significant other Mrs. Smith." I'd just divulged something personal, so I felt perfectly justified in getting a sliver of personal information from him. As it was, I hadn't asked him much except if he had any food allergies and if cotton blend sheets were all right.

He swept his hand through his thick hair. It did little to tame it. "There was a Mrs. Smith. She left me and I left her. It was sort of mutual." He chuckled quietly. "She just started packing her stuff in boxes, and I didn't stop her. That's how it ended."

"I'm sorry," I said for lack of a better response.

"Don't be. It was just a blip in my life. I've moved on and so has she. I think she just had twins." Nathaniel picked up his bowl. "Well, I think this pudding did the trick. I'm expecting heavy sleep once this noggin hits the pillow."

We stood up in unison. It was the closest we'd stood together. We stayed that way for a moment, nearly toe to toe, the familiar ticks and tocks of my kitchen appliances swirling around us. I couldn't tell who looked away first, but it seemed to be more on my side than his. I wondered if he realized that his blue gaze was unsettling... but not in a bad way. More like an 'Anna, get a hold of yourself' sort of way.

Nathaniel's white t-shirt stretched tightly over his back as he placed the bowl in the sink. He turned around and nodded. "Good night, Anna."

"Good night, Nate. Sleep tight."

"I'm planning on it."

twenty-two

IT SEEMED as if it had been weeks since I'd started the watercolor of the sweet pepperbush, but it had only been two days. The plant had had the good grace to stay exactly as I'd left it, with its layers of toothy, green leaves. Pink streaks across the horizon gave me just the light I needed to finish the piece. But I had to hurry before the sun popped up over the water and replaced the shadows with blinding light reflecting off the sea. Every artist had their favorite source of lighting. For me it was the unsteady light of Frostfall dawn or dusk. After my late night, I was sure I'd once again sleep through the alarm, but Huck was anticipating just that. He hated to miss our early morning walks in nature, so he made a point of waking me with a cold, wet nose to the back of my hand.

I always finished a watercolor by writing the name of the plant or animal or insect at the bottom of the piece in a fine black line. There was so much nature on the island, I never ran out of models. Although, it was much harder to paint a marsh fern moth than a wild geranium. Occasionally, I cheated and snapped a photo, a necessity when the model never sat still for longer than a few seconds, like the tiny, clear-winged blue dasher or a silver spotted skipper. It was the only way for me to catch the colors and nuances of the subject.

I sat back to survey my work. It wasn't bad but then again the model was as unwavering as a stone statue. I pulled out the banana I'd brought with me for a sunrise snack. As I unpeeled it and rested on my stool to wait for a glorious show of light from earth's favorite star, my walk companion jumped to his four paws and took off toward something behind me on the trail. There was a list of at least a dozen things he might be after, but I quickly discovered it was not the usual chickadee or mouse.

Nathaniel was wearing a sweatshirt, shorts and running shoes. "Looks like we both got the same amount of sleep." He glanced down at the artwork on my lap. "Wow, you're very talented."

"Thank you." I shut my tray of paints. "Did the pudding help?"

"I managed to finally doze off."

I got up from the stool.

"Do you need some help carrying stuff?" he asked. "I was heading that way, but I could help you back to the house."

"No, I've got a system." I tucked my paper and tray of paints under my arm and picked up the light stool.

Nathaniel glanced around at the scenery. "Are you ever worried? Being out here so early?"

"Worried about what? It's just me and nature."

"You mentioned how many murders happen on this island. Just thought maybe you'd want to be—"

"More careful? This is my home. I feel totally safe here."

"It is a beautiful place. It's hard to think of it as anything but safe. By the way, I didn't get a chance to tell you last night, I got a job here on the island."

"Did you? That's great. It's not easy to get a job here. Where is it at?" I realized I'd never really found out what he did for a living. Now it seemed I was going to have that answered.

"They're doing some construction on the northern lighthouse, some remodeling of the keeper's house. I'm going to be working on the construction crew."

"Wonderful. Yes, they've been anxious to get that project started. They were just waiting for winter to end." As we spoke, the sun lifted its bright face and began to wipe away the shadows on the island.

"I was thinking, since the northern lighthouse is a good distance away, I need to get a bike."

"That's probably a good idea. Burt's Bicycle Rentals on the wharf has some nice, gently used bikes for sale." It seemed we were finally having a normal, friendly chat and I was relieved. The job seemed to have improved his attitude. Feeling productive was part of being human.

"I'll head over there after breakfast. I start on Monday." A hint of a smile appeared. "Have to admit, I've never worked on a lighthouse. I'm looking forward to it."

"I can see that," I said teasingly. "I can make you a brown bag lunch like I do for Winston and Tobias."

"That'll be nice."

Huck barked to let me know we needed to get back and start breakfast. It was mostly his breakfast he was worried about. "I've got to get back to the house. Breakfast in an hour."

"I'll be back by then." He waved and turned to leave. I watched him jog away. His broad shoulders seemed far more relaxed than the first time I saw him. Maybe this hadn't been such a terrible mistake after all.

twenty-three

I'D MADE everyone's favorite buckwheat pancakes and heated the maple syrup and butter so that the toppings could cascade down the sides of the stack, but the mood at the table was mixed. Nathaniel had trailed in, smelling of the outdoors and a good run, just as everyone had started passing around the hot maple syrup. He said hello to the group and then carried his plate upstairs. That set everyone on edge. Opal complained that he thought himself too good to sit with us, but Tobias said he was just as happy not to have him at the table. Cora remained mostly quiet about the incident, but I sensed she was leaning toward Opal's side. Winston never stepped into debates unless it had to do with an animal, and I was on the fence. I would have liked Nathaniel to join us, to get to know all of us, but it seemed he needed more time. The job at the lighthouse would be a good first step.

In the meantime, I had to push aside the Moon River

drama. I had a case to solve. I tossed my phone and a notepad and pen into the white basket on the front of my bicycle. It was a beautiful spring day, made even more beautiful by the arrival of the first scarlet tanager. The bright red bird was always the first harbinger of new life on the island. Migrating birds would stop off to fatten up or nest before continuing north for the summer. The stout bird stood out red like a flame in the middle of the dark green, leathery leaves of the bayberry shrubs running along the front of the house. I snapped a photo, then climbed onto the bicycle.

My first stop was the Frostfall Historical Society and Maritime Museum. Abner Plunket, the man who ran the museum, knew everything about anyone who was associated with pirates. I was sure he would know Barry Long, a part-time resident on the island. Barry's position on the field and his generally distressed behavior about Arvin's death ranked him low on the suspect list. But I couldn't ignore a few glaring points. Barry was standing close enough to Arvin to shoot him in the temple. There was also motive. Arvin had lost a chunk of Barry's retirement in a bad investment scheme.

The brisk air cooled my cheeks and left my ears with a slight ache reminding me too late I should have worn a beanie or hat. Bright sunshine in spring was always misleading. My mind processed baby blue skies into visions of summer and sundresses and sandals, but the reality was that winter had not quite lost its glacial grip on the island. At least I hadn't let daydreams about lemonade and swims at the beach cloud my judgment on which sweater to wear for the bike ride. I paused to button up the soft peach cardigan before continuing my sprint to the museum.

Another sign that we were still just peeling out of a long winter was the lack of people lined up to enter the museum. Abner was very particular about his museum (technically, the museum belonged to the island, but he treated the place like it was his home). During the busy summer months, he limited the amount of visitors to twenty at a time. Sometimes, on a hot July day, when tourists coated the boardwalk and the beaches, the line would wrap all the way to the Pirate's Gold restaurant. And Jack Drake, the owner, would take advantage of the foot traffic by offering brown bag lunches filled with roasted chicken sandwiches and homemade oatmeal raisin cookies. Tourists would stand in line, nibbling their goodies while waiting for their turn in the museum. Abner, who was persnickety by nature, liked to complain to Jack that the visitors would all be entering with greasy fingers, but Jack told him if his line was going to stretch to the restaurant, then he was going to serve food.

Abner Plunkett was just pulling a chalkboard sign advertising the special price for summer passes onto the sidewalk. Abner was a small, fast moving man whose shoes always seemed too big for his feet. He had fuzz instead of hair. His wife, Rita, was a retired school teacher, and the couple shared a small Victorian cottage on the north end of Island Drive. The unwieldy double-sided chalkboard sign got stuck on the doorjamb. I parked my bike and hurried over to help him.

I startled him in the process when, for no apparent reason, the sign suddenly moved freely out of the doorway.

"Anna," he said on a breath mixed with a laugh. "I didn't see you there. I thought I'd suddenly gained a big burst of strength in these old man muscles."

"Sorry to pop that bubble."

We dragged the sign along the front of the museum. The early century, saltbox style building had two newly added wings (built to match the original version). Years earlier, it had been the town library, slash pharmacy, slash soda shop. The town doctor, a man who traveled by horseback along the dirt trail that was now Island Drive, had an office right next to the soda counter. I'd heard stories of how people would be sitting enjoying their egg salad sandwiches and ginger ales as a patient was yelling in agony while getting an ingrown toenail removed. Once the town had decided to go all in on the unfounded pirate stories, they realized they needed a place to showcase the island's rich swashbuckling history. The wings had been added to house the pirate scenes, displays that were more suited to a carnival or amusement park than a museum. Children particularly liked the south addition where the entire space was made to resemble the deck of a pirate ship complete with ship's wheel, rope rigging and crew bunks. (Automaton pirates slept in the bunks and woke sporadically to yell out Ahoy matey, dead men tale no tales and other buccaneer classics.)

After a few minutes of moving the sign to and fro, side to side, as if we were trying to decide exactly where to place a new sofa, Abner was satisfied with the position. "I'm hoping we get a lot of passes sold this summer. The funds help us stay open in the off season." His cheeks were red from moving the sign. "What brings you out here this morning?" His smile fell. "I'm sure you heard all about the terrible tragedy at the pirate reenactment. We'd all been so excited about it, but I doubt the group will choose Frostfall Island next year."

"That's actually why I'm here, Abner. I was hoping you could help me. How well do you know Barry Long?"

Abner's thin brows popped up in surprise. "Barry? You don't think he had anything to do with this, do you? He's a genuinely nice guy, ole Barry."

"No, I'm just trying to get a little background on all the people who were standing in the area where Meeks was shot. It's process of elimination. Barry's character of Captain Morgan was on the field, and his job in the battle was to take down the Spaniard, Arvin Meeks. I don't think Barry had anything to do with the murder, but I was hoping to talk to him about it. He was pretty shaken up yesterday, so I thought he'd be more receptive to questions today. Do you happen to know if he's on the island?"

"From what I've heard, the numbskull Norwich (generally, a lot of nicknames showed fondness or admiration like with a beloved pet but not in Norwich's case) told everyone involved with the reenactment they needed to stay local. Since the tents were already set up for the weekend most everyone was staying up at North Pond."

"Can I find Barry there?" I was hoping to get the man alone. A busy campsite was not going to make that easy.

"No, you won't find Barry at the camp. He owns a little beach house near the swimming beach."

I snapped my fingers. "That's right. Molly mentioned that when she introduced me to Barry at the produce stand." I shook my head. "Boy, you turn forty one minute and the next your whole memory has turned to Swiss cheese."

Abner laughed. "Wait until sixty. Then you'll be asking yourself what is Swiss cheese?"

"Do you know Barry's address? I hate to start knocking on all the beach cottage doors."

"Uh, again, because I'm sixty, specific addresses are no longer part of my memory bank, but his house is white with bright blue trim and he has the nicest Japanese Honeysuckle plant in front of the porch. It's fourth or fifth from the swimming beach. You can't miss it. I think you'll quickly take him off the suspect list. He's a grand guy, that Barry. That's why they asked him to be Morgan. He's got all the swagger and charm needed to be a pirate captain."

"Thanks for the information, and good luck with your summer pass sale." I waved and headed back to my bike. It was time to talk to the notorious Captain Morgan.

twenty-four

USING ABNER'S DIRECTIONS, Barry's house was easy to find. Especially because Barry himself was out in the front yard, pruning the honeysuckle bush. Abner was right. It was lovely.

Barry was crouched down and stooped over, yet he still looked bigger than most men. My squeaky bike brakes alerted him to my arrival.

He glanced over his big, round shoulder, lifted his sunglasses and squinted across the yard. He grinned and groaned as he pushed to his feet. "Anna," he said, "what brings you this way?" His grin vanished. "Have they caught the culprit?"

"Not yet." I strolled up the stepping stones leading to the front stoop of his cottage. It overlooked the soft sand of the swimming beach, a prime piece of real estate in island terms. "What a cute place and what a location."

He glanced back to admire his small white cottage. With

its straight edged corners and shallow roof it could almost be considered a shack rather than a cottage. Either way, I had no doubt it was homey inside. "Yes, when she came on the market, I didn't even hesitate." He turned back to me.

I shielded my eyes and gazed up at him like I was looking at a tall tree. "I'm here about the case."

"Thought you might be." He pulled off his sunglasses and wiped them on his shirt. He stuck them back on, grunted and pulled them back off. "I fall for it every time. I think my shirt is going to give them a nice shine, but they only get worse." He stuck the glasses in his pocket. "What can I do for you? I'm eager to share anything that helps. I'm just not sure I have much."

"I'll be blunt, Barry. I don't think you killed Arvin."

His face went through a series of contortions before finally landing on a weak smile. "That's good to hear especially because I had nothing to do with Arvin's death. I'm one of those silly saps who carries a spider outside rather than wash it down the sink like normal people."

I laughed lightly. "Then I'm not normal either because I do the same thing. Unless it's a really big spider, then I just let it find its own way out. That said, there are a few things that sort of highlight you on the persons of interest list."

His earlier smile faded. "Because I was the one who shot him on the battlefield. But the gun was a prop, a harmless cap gun. The props are elaborate replicas. The explosion and smoke is generated by a cap."

"I think the assailant had a real gun hiding in their costume," I noted. "The prop guns were all accounted for, including the one Captain Morgan was assigned. But, Barry, there's the matter of Arvin losing your money."

Barry motioned toward the shade of his front stoop. As we headed that direction, he pulled out his phone. "Let me show you something, something that will put that whole money issue quickly to rest." He thumbed through his screen for something. I couldn't think what he might be trying to show me. I was even more confused when he turned the phone toward me. A gleaming dark gold truck was sitting on a paved driveway.

I glanced up at him. "I don't know much about cars, but is that a vintage El Camino?"

"Yup, a '72 in mint condition. It belonged to Arvin. I admired the truck for years. After he lost my money, he gifted me the El Camino. The monetary value didn't equal what I lost, but I'd been wanting that truck for so long, I didn't mind. It's sitting in my garage at home waiting to go for a cruise." He put the phone away. "So you see, as disappointed as I was with Arvin, he more than made up for it."

"I'm glad that worked out for you. It is a beautiful truck. Since you've had a day to replay yesterday's event in your mind, did anything pop up? Anything that might help us find the killer?"

Barry shook his head. "Just like you said, I've replayed the whole thing again and again. There was so much chaos and so many people. I just don't know who fired that shot."

"I'll let you get back to your garden. It's promising to be a fabulous spring," I said as I walked back to my bike.

"Can't wait."

twenty-five

I LEANED my bicycle against the thick gray trunk of a white pine and started toward the tents. A head of wavy blond hair made it easy to pick Deke Silverton out of the crowd milling about the campsite. People were settled under trees, nibbling goodies on picnic blankets and strolling along the bank of the pond. The enthusiasm and general merriment of the day before was gone, and the mood, while not as somber as one might expect, was definitely subdued.

Deke was sipping a soda and glancing at some paperwork as I walked up. "Excuse me," I said to get his attention.

Sunlight reflected off the mirrored lenses of his sunglasses. He caught me squinting as the bright light shot back toward me and pushed the glasses up into the cloud of blond hair.

"I'm sorry to bother you. I'm Anna St. James." I stuck out my hand and we shook.

"Right, you were here yesterday helping out after the

murder." He had piercing gunmetal gray eyes. "Are you with that detective? I didn't get his name, but he spoke to some of us, the people who were on the field near Arvin." I was surprised Norwich took the time to talk to people or even find out who was on the field. "I'm not sure if I have anything else to say that would help the case. I just hope you get the person soon." I took the statement to mean he was worried about a killer running around on the loose, but I soon found his concern lay elsewhere. "The detective ordered us all to stay here on the island until he made an arrest. I've got to get back to town for a commercial audition." He lifted the papers in his hand. A quick glance showed that it was a script.

"Oh, you're an actor," I said. My only interest in Deke was that he was one of the role players standing to the left of Meeks during the battle. I hoped the casual interview would reveal whether there was any connection between the two men other than that they both participated in reenactments.

"I can't make a living doing this." He glanced around at the camp. The costume and refreshment tents billowed in the gentle ocean breeze. That same breeze sent ripples across the lush grass and the surface of the pond.

"No, I suppose not," I added.

"The role playing events let me practice my craft. I joined this one just a few months ago. I usually participate in medieval and civil war reenactments but I thought a pirate one would be fun." His sunglasses shimmied in his hair as he shook his head. "Boy, was I wrong. This one turned out to be a catastrophe. I mean, we're out there shooting at each other and playing dead, but no one is supposed to actually die. It's crazy and creepy."

"Not exactly what any of us spectators had in mind either. Since you just joined the group, I assume you didn't know the victim too well."

"Nope, just like I told that toothpick eating detective, only met him a few times when we were rehearsing for the battle."

I had to stifle the laugh he'd stirred up with his toothpick comment. "So you don't know of anyone who had a problem with Meeks?"

"Only that whole thing about him losing people's money." As he spoke, I spotted Alan Jessup walking across to his costume tent. He was my next interview.

"Thanks for talking to me. I hope you get the part." I looked pointedly at the script as I passed him.

I picked up my pace and opened the flap on the costume tent. Jessup was hanging costumes on a rack.

"Hello," I called. "Do you mind if I come inside?"

Jessup glanced up from his task. "That's fine as long as you don't mind if I keep hanging these costumes. The humidity is starting to ruin them."

"Absolutely. I appreciate your time."

Jessup hung a quilted doublet on a hanger and put it on the rack. "The detective glanced at the papers I showed you, the lists and battlefield schematic drawing, but he was more interested in hearing what I knew about Barry Long. Which wasn't all that much." He paused his work and looked at me. "Do you think Barry killed Arvin?"

"I don't. Unfortunately, Detective Norwich always jumps on the easiest target. Barry was near the victim, and in the battle scenario he was supposed to kill Arvin. I'm sure he just decided Barry did it."

Jessup picked up a white drop sleeve shirt and began folding it. "He told us we all needed to stay on the island until he made an arrest. He expected that to be very soon. Of course, we all thought we'd be here until Sunday. Tonight we were supposed to have a pirate's victory feast. There's plenty of food for everyone through the weekend, but after that, people are going to be anxious to leave. We've all got jobs and families on the mainland."

"I know you're busy, but I need to ask you something." I knew the next question would make him bristle, but sometimes I had to just go for it.

"What's that?" There was already a little hardness in his tone.

"You mentioned you hardly knew Meeks. Was it true he was your financial consultant? Did he lose your money?"

A loud, puffy sigh followed as he placed a pirate vest back down on the heap. "I stand by my first answer. I didn't know him well. I hardly ever talked to him except to hand him his costume. I was his client, but we only spoke a few times through email and once on the phone. That was all purely business." Spring weather was starting to seep into the tent making the air inside warm and humid. Jessup rolled up the sleeves of his shirt. "He lost some of my money. I'm more embarrassed than angry. When I set out to buy something like a dishwasher, I do hours of research, read every review, compare all the prices. But with my retirement fund, which is small, believe me, I tossed the paltry sum I had into Arvin's hands without even checking on his credentials. Barry had recommended him, and I liked Barry so that was all I needed. Big regret. But again, it was such a small sum, it wasn't all that devastating. Just disappointing."

"Why didn't you mention that you were his client when I asked how well you knew him?"

"For all the reasons I just said. I was ashamed at how careless I'd been, and I really didn't know the guy. How well do know your financial planner?" It was a good question.

I smiled weakly. "I know his full name and I think he has two cats, but you're right, I wouldn't recognize him if he was standing next to me at the grocery store. But then, we aren't in the same reenactment group either."

"Good point but since I'm in here, I don't interact with the role players much. That reminds me—something that might interest you. I was thinking back to all the time leading up to the battle and something popped out at me, something I'd forgotten about until this morning. One of the papers you photographed contained a list of role players. I keep a spreadsheet of all the names so I know who has what costume and prop. The morning we were setting up camp, Arvin came to my tent looking a little red in the face and upset." He shook his head. "Again, I don't know why this just occurred to me. I guess I've been so busy and then with the murder and the police—" he waved his hand to stop his tangent. "Anyhow, Arvin wanted to see the list of people participating in the reenactment. It wasn't a 'hey, let's see who's out here this weekend' kind of request. He looked serious, and if I thought about it, a little worried."

"Do you think he was looking for a specific name?" I asked.

"Yes. He dragged his finger down the list like someone might do if they were searching for something specific. He got to the bottom, shook his head, muttered something to himself and then handed me back the list. I asked him if he found the person he was looking for? He just grunted and walked out of the tent. It wasn't like Arvin at all. He was always pleasant, polite. He felt really bad about losing my money and insisted he'd repay me. Never saw the money, but I had no reason to doubt that he'd give it back eventually."

My intuition told me Arvin's unusual request to scan the participant list was important. "Did you tell Detective Norwich about Arvin's interest in the list?"

"No, like I said, it just came to me this morning. I guess I should, but to tell you the truth, he mostly only had questions about Barry Long. He wasn't too pleased when I kept saying that Barry was a nice guy who would never hurt anyone. Seemed like he didn't want to hear that."

I shook my head. "I'm sure he didn't because you were messing up his simple one-step investigation. Zero in on the most likely culprit, find scanty evidence to charge the person and haul them in."

Jessup returned to his task of folding linen shirts. "He's not exactly a Columbo, is he? Although, I was sure I spotted some mustard on his tie, and his coat looked wrinkly, even wet from the rain."

"That's probably the only similarities between them. Thanks so much for your help."

"No problem. I just hope this gets resolved soon. I hate to think we're eating lunch in the mess tent with a killer passing around the salt or a napkin."

"Does make for an uneasy meal," I said on my way out of the tent.

twenty-six

I LINGERED around the camp for awhile, hoping to overhear conversations and pluck out anything I could find that related to the case. It seemed most people were focused on getting off the island and back home. The event had huge promise of excitement and merriment, but it ended with a bang... literally. Unfortunately it was impossible to hear the bang over all the sound effects.

I was just about to head back to the white pine where I'd left my bicycle when Sarah, the red headed woman Barry Long had pointed out as one of Arvin's *special* friends hurried across the grass on a pair of pink flip-flops. Since I was standing alone in the spot she was heading, I could only assume she was frantically shuffling over to see me.

"You're the lady who was helping with Arvin's—" She stopped both to catch her breath and to swallow, as if just talking about him was painful. "I'm sorry. It's just that I'm still having such a hard time believing this is real. Wake me up, do you know what I mean?" she laughed faintly.

"Yes, I'm sure it's been a terrible shock. Were you close with Mr. Meeks?"

"Very. We've been seeing each other off and on for a year. Thought we might even get married eventually but you know how reluctant men are to tie the knot these days." She was one of those women who could instantly drop into a girl chat, where she made it seem as if you'd known her for years. "But I guess that's not happening now," she added darkly. "Is it true you're an investigator? I've always thought it would be fun to be a private eye, you know, wear the fedora and trench coat, maybe some bright blue kitten heels, practical but just stylish enough to throw people off so they don't realize you're a private eye."

"I think dropping the fedora and trench coat might be a better place to start the whole incognito thing but then who doesn't love a nice trench coat. To answer your question, I am sort of the unofficial investigator on this island. I pick up where the professionals leave holes." That was a beauty of an understatement.

Sarah sidled closer to me. Her eyes were a vivid blue, nearly matching the sky above. She was petite and a few inches shorter, so I had to lean down when she dropped her voice lower. "I don't know if this has come out yet but someone in the group is an experienced marksman. Or in this case, a markswoman. And she was on the field when the battle started." She paused and glanced around at the campsite. People were strolling across to the refreshment tent. Some were leaving with what appeared to be root beer floats. The bubbly concoctions seemed to be the reason for the stream of people heading to the food tent.

"Her name is Evie Stern," Sarah continued.

It took a moment for the familiarity to take hold. (It seemed forty years was turning me into my parents.) Evie was the sporty looking tavern wench Arvin had shared a chai tea with on the morning before the event. I quickly reminded myself that I would have to take everything Sarah said about Evie with some caution. If the two women knew about each other, they were most certainly not friends. Still, the information she'd just handed me was compelling.

Naturally, I kept up the pretense that I knew nothing about Arvin's *other* woman. "This woman, Evie Stern, can you point her out to me?"

Sarah pulled her sunglasses on to give the area a scan without letting people know she was looking at them. After a few seconds, she shook her head. "I don't see her right now. She is early forties with auburn hair and very nice lips. Although personally, I think they're a little large for her face. She was dressed as a tavern wench for the reenactment."

"Ah yes, I think I know who you're talking about. She's an expert markswoman?"

"She's got a bunch of awards and everything. She always brags that she could shoot a wart off a witch's nose." Evie lightly touched her chest. "Now, I'm not accusing anyone, of course."

"Of course." Although, it sure came pretty darn close to an accusation.

"I just thought it should be known. People were saying that Arvin was hit right in the temple. One of those shots that was meant to kill." She paused and pressed her fingers to her lips for a moment. "And kill it did." The last words were quiet and broken up. She added in a few exaggerated eye blinks as if holding back tears, but I didn't see any. "Still can't believe it." She took a deep breath. "Anyhow, I thought you might want to know. I tried to tell that silly detective, but he seemed more interested in getting out of the rain than hearing important details."

"Yes, that sounds like Detective Norwich. I appreciate you taking the time to tell me this. I'll put it in my notes."

Sarah grinned and seemed quite pleased with herself. "We need to find out who killed poor Arvin. He just didn't deserve to die." The lashes blinked over perceived tears, yet again.

"I agree. Thanks for your time." I reached my bike. The sun was peaked in the sky. A pair of robins had landed in the white pine. They watched me with great bird curiosity as I pulled my bike out from under their branch. They'd started a scraggly nest in a fork between two branches, and it seemed my presence had stopped the construction.

I pushed the bike out onto Island Drive. It was getting close to noon. I needed to get back home and start the grilled cheese sandwiches I'd planned for lunch.

twenty-seven

I'D BARELY REACHED the front steps of the house when my phone rang. It was my friend, Mindy, at the city precinct. I sat down on the step to talk to her. With any luck, she had some insider information about the case.

"Hey, Mindy, how are you? It's been awhile."

"It has. How was the fortieth? Mine is just around the corner, and I'm dreading it."

"Around the corner? I thought you were a few years younger than me."

"Well, a few years around the corner anyhow. Who looks back once you pass that thirty-five year mark? Did you have a big party?"

"Nothing too big. Seraphina baked a cake."

"I miss her blueberry tarts. I need to get over to the island. Then we can sit with a cup of tea and catch up."

"That sounds great, Mindy." I could hear the usual businesslike noises of the precinct, phones ringing, voices, both agitated and calm, in the background. "Since you're calling, I assume you heard that we had another Frostfall murder."

She laughed dryly. "Sure did. I wasn't all that surprised to hear."

"I know. Our reputation as the murder capital of the Atlantic prevails. This time it even included some pirates. The island's founders would be thrilled." I realized how crazy that sounded, but they were all a little pirate obsessed.

I heard some papers shuffling. "Don't know if you know this considering you're usually on top of everything that has to do with these unfortunate events, but Norwich is making an arrest."

"Hmm, let me guess. Barry Long?"

She huffed. "See, just when I think I've got something juicy to tell you, you out juice me by knowing exactly what I'm going to say."

I laughed. "Sorry about that. Next time I'll play dumb."

"I don't think you could be dumb even if you were pretending. Anyhow, here's the crazy part that even I can see as wrong. Not surprising considering who is behind the warrant. The coroner retrieved the bullet from the victim's brain. It was shot from a Ruger GP100. With a minor bit of research, Norwich discovered that Barry Long owns a Ruger GP100. So do hundreds of thousands of other people, but that didn't stop Norwich. When they got to the island to make the arrest, Barry let them search his cottage because he said the gun was not on the island but securely tucked in a gun safe at his home here in town."

"Which makes it impossible for Barry to have used that

handgun in a murder that happened here on the island yesterday afternoon," I finished.

"Exactly. It's a flimsy case, but that never stops Buckston Norwich from getting his man," she mused.

"Even if it's the wrong man." Behind me, inside the house, I could hear Opal and Cora discussing lunch and the fact that it was late. "I've got to go, Mindy. Thanks for calling. This is all good stuff."

"You bet, and let's plan that cup of tea soon."

"Absolutely." I hung up and got to my feet. I had quite a bit of information to add to the chart. Since Norwich's hunches were almost universally wrong, I knew I could put Barry Long at the bottom of my list of suspects.

twenty-eight

WHILE NORWICH WAS BEING PAID to dedicate his full work day to the investigation, I still had a day job running the boarding house. After lunch, where a plan to watch a movie outside was hatched over grilled cheese and slices of dill pickle, I'd spent a good hour dusting and vacuuming the front room, a place with some old cozy furniture, bookshelves and a salty, comforting aroma that came through the large picture window. It was a place we liked to play cards or read books, one of everyone's favorite common rooms aside from the kitchen.

After my cleaning spree, I'd cut potatoes and carrots for a chunky vegetable pot pie and iced a pan of brownies for the evening movie before finally carving out some time to list my new information on the corkboards. A few cases back, Tobias had suggested using different colored index cards to list details for each suspect. Barry Long was green. I wrote down the information Mindy had given me. He owned a Ruger

GP100, the same kind of gun that was used to kill Arvin. Even though it was all a huge farce, like most things coming from Norwich, I added that Barry had in fact been arrested for the murder. I also noted the gun that was supposedly used for the killing had been nowhere near the actual murder site but instead locked away in a gun safe across the channel. I'd texted Frannie after lunch to make sure Barry hadn't gone home on the ferry anytime between Friday afternoon and this afternoon. Just as I expected, Barry never left the island. If he had managed to get his gun on Friday and just as quickly get it back to the gun safe on Saturday, it would have meant he had an accomplice. That seemed like a stretch.

Deke Silverton was yellow in my card cataloguing. There wasn't much to say except I made note he was an actor who only recently joined the group to practice his craft. However, considering his short time with the group, he knew about the financial scandal and that Arvin had lost some of the fellow participants' retirement funds. I stared at the card after I pinned it under the Deke Silverton stick figure. How many other people did Arvin hurt with his bad investment? Who was Arvin looking for on the list? Could the killer be someone from outside the group? How would they have been on the field in costume? The spectators were far enough away that early on I'd set to rest any notion that the gun was fired from somewhere on the perimeter of the battlefield. It seemed impossible to shoot into an active scene where the players were running to and fro, firing off prop guns, swinging fake cutlasses and still hit the target. Even for someone with expert aim.

Which brought me to the peach colored cards I'd set aside for Evie Stern. I wrote down that Sarah informed me Evie was an expert markswoman who had won awards and bragged about how good she was. I added in witch's wart to remind me of the cute phrase she used. I highlighted the name Sarah to remind myself that the information had not been confirmed. I starred the name as a reminder that Sarah and Evie were both seeing Arvin Meeks.

I stepped back to admire my multi-colored board. I had some good information. Now, if I could just find the piece that would help me connect the killer to the victim. There were still too many holes.

For now, I had to take off my sleuthing cap and pull on my boarding house apron. I'd decided the lovely spring weather should be celebrated with a big hearty salad. That meant I had a lot of peeling, chopping and grating to do. And baking because you couldn't truly enjoy a healthy salad without a fresh buttery roll to accompany it.

twenty-nine

TWO CHRISTMASES AGO, we'd pooled our money together to buy the entire house a present, a large roll-up movie screen and a projector. We'd all dreamt of summer movie nights out under the stars. The whole set-up grew more elaborate when the following year we pooled our money and purchased large comfy bean bags to sit on while munching popcorn and enjoying one of our favorite movie classics. The bean bags were certainly fun and comfy, but we did realize too late that they were unwieldy to move in and out of the house and storing them for winter took a lot of space. So the whole thing got even more elaborate when we pooled our money to buy a small storage shed for our outdoor theater. More storage room meant adding a popcorn cart and goodies table to the mix. We did however draw the line at the professional theater quality speakers Winston had suggested. We didn't want to scare off the wildlife.

A sliver of a moon hung overhead as the popcorn cart

popped the yellow kernels into perfect white puffs. Was there ever a more familiar scent than popcorn? Huck had already settled himself in front of the cart so he could catch anything that fell. Winston, the official tech guy, mostly because he was the youngest and, as was always the case, the most tech savvy, finished setting up the projector and laptop. It was Cora's turn to pick the movie, and she'd decided on "Some Like it Hot". I had placed buttercream frosted brownies on plates and cold milk in cups. We always kept a supply of movie theater candy on hand for movie night because what was a good classic movie without a red licorice vine or box of chocolate covered peanuts?

I'd pulled out the extra bean bag for our newest tenant, but I wasn't expecting him to show up. Balancing my brownie and my milk, I settled into my bean chair without spilling or losing a crumb. Tobias had been grumbling about the movie choice, but he finally decided it was as good as any and frosted brownies would make the whole thing easier to watch.

We were all settled in watching the opening credits and nibbling our brownies when the back door opened. Nathaniel walked out. Eyes were now focused on Mr. Smith rather than Lemmon and Curtis. He strolled over to the table, picked up a brownie and a red licorice, then headed over to the open bean bag chair. I hadn't really planned that the open chair would be right next to me. That was just how it landed. Cora, a few bags away, looked slyly my direction as if I'd planned it. The truth was, I thought there was more of a chance of Jack Lemmon sitting in that empty chair than our new housemate, and last I checked, Lemmon had been dead for a few decades.

Nathaniel was wearing a blue flannel shirt that matched his eyes. His sleeves were rolled back. The whole look worked for him, but I doubted there were too many *looks* that wouldn't work. He motioned to the empty bean bag. "This seat taken?"

"Not unless Jack Lemmon shows up, then you're on your own." I had no idea why the silliness popped out. It just did.

He chuckled as he easily lowered himself into the bag as if just sitting on a bench. "This one has Marilyn Monroe, right?"

"Yes."

"Nice," he said in a typical man response to the prospect of seeing Marilyn Monroe.

Huck noticed the newest addition to the theater. He hopped up to his big paws, trotted over and flopped down next to Nathaniel's bag.

"I think you just rated higher than popcorn on Huck's favorite things list," I noted. "I, myself, the woman who feeds, bathes and buys his squeaky toys that he annihilates in twenty minutes am still below popcorn on the list."

Nathaniel smiled at the dog. "I'll bet if that was a hot dog cart rather than a popcorn cart, we'd be having a whole different conversation." He leaned his head closer so he could talk without getting shushed. Opal was the main shusher on movie night, even though she knew every line of script from every movie ever made before 1950. "Your corkboards are impressive," he said on a half whisper. "The color coding was a great idea."

I leaned my head and realized we were close enough that I could smell his aftershave, a nice, warm, woodsy scent. "The color coding was Tobias' idea. And thanks. I just wish I had more to go on."

"I noticed one of the cards said an arrest was made. Do you think they've got the wrong guy?" Up until that point, we'd been watching the screen as we talked, but I turned my face toward him. He did the same. We were nearly nose to nose. I waited for him to pull back. He didn't. I moved back first.

"You read the cards?" I asked.

"I'm sorry. They are out on display. I thought they were for anyone to read."

"No, I'm not mad. I'm just surprised they would interest you."

He leaned his head to the side teasingly. "I just like to know exactly what kind of crazy place I settled in." A grin followed.

"Don't look too closely. You might just pack your things right back up."

"Is that another attempt to push me out the door?" He picked up a brownie. "Cuz your cooking and baking are going to make that harder than you think." He took a bite and a low, appreciative moan followed. "So good."

"Thank you. I'd like to take credit for inventing the box brownie, but all I did was add eggs and oil."

"The frosting?" he asked as he licked some off his thumb.

"That's all mine."

"See and that's the best part."

I couldn't deny that I was lapping up the compliments about my culinary skills. It was always nice to be appreciated.

"So, the detective with the mustard stain has the wrong guy?" he asked, reviving our pre-brownie topic.

"Lots of weak evidence and the guy he pulled in didn't really have a motive. There was a little scuffle about a financial mishap, but it was all taken care of when the victim gave him his prized El Camino to make up for it."

I had no idea why but for a long, ridiculous moment I watched his muscular forearms as he held his brownie plate. "I don't think I could kill a man who gifted me his El Camino. What year?" he asked.

"A '72 in mint condition."

He closed his eyes, dropped his head back and made a moaning sound similar to the one used for the brownie. "Oh man, nope I'd never kill that guy. Norwich has the wrong man."

"My intuition tells me so," I said.

His soft chuckle was starting to become a familiar sound. I liked it. "So you're out here on this remote island solving murders with colorful index cards, stick figures and your intuition?"

"The others help," I added, lamely.

"Of course. I should have listed that."

I turned slightly to face him but realized right then and there mushy bean bag chairs were not great when you wanted to turn to someone and make a point. My whole body sort of slipped right back into the original hole my bottom made when I first sat down.

"Mr. Smith, are you mocking my investigation?" I was pretending to be amused, but, in fact, I was slightly hurt.

"Not at all. I think it's impressive." We hadn't realized that our voices had reached normal pitch until Opal shushed us.

We both scooted down instinctively, a sort of knee-jerk reaction as if sinking lower would make our voices less audible.

"Here's the thing about solving murders," he started in a more hushed tone. "It all works fine if you can pin all the evidence and a motive on the killer. But if there is no motive—let's say the killer is a homicidal maniac who kills randomly. If the murderer's sole motive is the desire to kill, then that makes catching the monster much harder."

I sat quietly absorbing what he said. All of it was true and made perfect sense, but why on earth had he brought up the phrase homicidal maniac? Thus far, the mishaps on the island had been for a reason, a personal squabble, jealousy, or money. For some, it was an obvious lapse of judgment, whether an impulsive act or a carefully laid out plan. None of the people brought to justice on Frostfall Island had serial killer tendencies. Had that changed? Was he trying to confess something? There it was again—that darn pebble. It had disappeared entirely, and I was sure it was gone for good, then boom, it was back under my heel, letting me know it hadn't left my shoe. I needed to at least give the shoe a little shake, or I would, once again, toss and turn all night.

"You seem to know a lot about murders." I ignored the

shushing coming from Opal. This was more important than Tony Curtis in a dress.

"Do I?" he asked with a wry smile. "Guess I watch too many of those cop shows on television." He pushed the last piece of brownie in and stuck the red vine into his mouth, letting it dangle there like a limp cigarette. "Well, Marilyn or not, this is probably not my kind of movie." He exited the chair with the same annoying grace as when he sat in it. "Good night, Anna."

"Good night, Nate."

Darn pebble.

thirty

AS EXPECTED, my somewhat unsettling chat with Nathaniel had put a good night's sleep out of reach. (I was still struggling with whether or not it was actually unsettling. Murder was always an odd topic.)

Since I was wide awake, I carried a cup of hot apple and cinnamon tea, a leftover from fall, up to my room. Nathaniel Smith might have been a common name, but I was sure the name Arvin Meeks was going to have far more manageable results. Sometimes, when I was stuck on a case, I found a dive into the past could churn up new information.

The first result was his business website, Arvin Meeks Finances. I clicked on it and found that he hadn't updated the site for several months. That wasn't unusual and neither was anything else on the page. He did promise people that he'd "do right by their money". It was a mission statement that was repeated throughout the site. Seemed he'd broken that promise. Now it was a moot point since he wouldn't be doing right by anyone's money anymore.

The next result was an article about the sketchy financial scheme that Meeks and at least a dozen other financial planners had gotten caught up in. It seemed lots of people lost retirement funds, and a class action suit was still pending.

There was, interestingly enough, another Arvin Meeks who owned a pet store in Iowa. He had recently won an award for best shop in his small town.

Farther down, my keywords 'Arvin Meeks' were bolded in an article about a hometown tragedy. I clicked on it. Someone had scanned in a somewhat faded photo of six boys standing arm in arm in front of a lake. I was no expert, but on first glance it seemed the boys ranged in age from around twelve to sixteen. They were barefoot, in swim trunks and they all wore that suntanned, windswept, carefree look most kids wore in the middle of summer vacation.

I had only seen Arvin briefly, as he sipped tea and smiled charmingly at his date and on the battlefield, both dead and alive, but there was something about the big dark eyes of the kid in the middle of the photo that assured me I was looking at Arvin in his youth. The newspaper had labeled the boys from left to right, the same way a school yearbook would be written. Midnight bleary eyes or not, I'd been right about Arvin Meeks, the boy in the middle.

The other names were not familiar. Two of the boys, the youngest looking one on the right and a tall, older boy on the left shared the same last name, Dickson. Pete Dickson must have been the younger brother of James Dickson because not only did they share the same surname, they also shared the same smile. James was definitely heading into manhood, and Pete was still on that awkward ledge between childhood and the teen years.

I scanned the article and quickly discovered it was not about cherry popsicles, swimming, sunburned noses and all the other joys of summer. Instead, it grimly told about an accident. The photo must have been the only one the journalist could get his hands on showing all the boys involved in the tragedy. It seemed the six boys had decided to jump a freight train as it shambled along the tracks near their homes. One boy, the older brother, James Dickson, had jumped onboard but then worried his younger brother Pete wasn't going to make it. James jumped back out to help his brother and that was when the wheel caught him and dragged him beneath train. The other boys looked on in horror as their friend died a terrible death.

I leaned back and closed my eyes. It wasn't what I'd expected to read before trying to fall asleep. I collected myself and opened my eyes. Before I could click out of the article, I scanned the smiling faces in the photo. It compounded the sadness of the story, six good friends doing something that was admittedly foolhardy but then wasn't that part of being young? Arvin had suffered an awful loss as a youth, but I couldn't see how the incident would have any bearing on his murder. The article was twenty-five years old, a lot of time and healing had passed.

I clicked out of the article, but as the photo disappeared, a pair of eyes suddenly looked familiar. They didn't belong to

Arvin Meeks. As much as I wanted to put the article behind me, I opened it again. It was the younger Dickson brother, Pete Dickson. There was something about the way he gazed at the camera that gave me déjà vu. I'd seen that gaze, those eyes before. But where?

"Argh, curse you forty. If I was still thirty-nine it would have popped right into my head." I stared at the laptop and considered doing some more research about the Pillow Talk Killer but then I'd probably never sleep again.

I closed the laptop and rested against the pillow I'd propped up behind me. After Nathaniel had left the movie, Cora hoisted (not an exaggeration considering she was wearing a tight pair of pants and sitting in a bean bag) herself to her feet. She came over to sit next to me. She told me she wanted to share her box of Junior Mints, like old times, to which I reminded her she rarely shared anything with me when we were kids. Just seconds after plopping into the seat and pouring two measly mints onto my palm, she dove right into her real motive for moving. She wanted to know what Nathaniel and I spoke about. She insisted that I looked slightly distressed about the conversation. I still hadn't mentioned the Pillow Talk Killer articles in Nathaniel's room to anyone. I had no plans to either. At least, not until I had more information to go with it. Unfortunately, I'd been uncharacteristically timid with Mr. Smith. Part of that was because I didn't want to bring up the humiliation of being caught snooping in his room. I told Cora she'd misread my expression and that my distress came from trying to decide whether to have some chocolate covered peanuts or another brownie. She didn't believe me, but she also did nudge further.

While sucking on the mint, I resolved to find out why Nathaniel was so interested in the PTK. But first, I needed to find out who killed Arvin Meeks.

thirty-one

NORMALLY, Sunday breakfast was waffles topped with whatever fresh fruit was in season. I had planned to make buttermilk waffles with sliced bananas and warm strawberry syrup, but my housemates had eaten themselves silly with brownies and movie treats. Opal described it as a Tony Curtis and sugar hangover. Too much of both. She and Cora both requested black coffee for breakfast. Even the thought of cream was too much. Tobias, who was always much more prudent about his sweet intake, said he'd be fine with popping a few slices of bread in the toaster after his swim. Winston was up and ready for a meal, but when he noticed no one else was eating, he told me they were carrying his favorite jalapeño cheese bagels at the coffee kiosk on the boardwalk and he'd eat there. He was just being polite because I caught a hint of a waffle-less Sunday frown as he left. That left only one tenant, and since Nathaniel seemed to be sleeping late, I left a note that there was bread, jam and hardboiled eggs in the fridge. Since I had a touch of the sugar hangover and not enough sleep to go with it, I decided to take the morning off and stroll on the beach. With any luck, I'd find a nice shell to paint.

With straw hat in hand, I took off at a brisk clip toward Chicory Trail and Thousand Step Beach. The early morning sun had lifted gracefully above the horizon, and the ocean sparkled as if someone had sprinkled it with diamonds.

Huck pranced ahead, nose in the air, which meant either he was onto a squirrel or Olive was cooking bacon this morning. The way his nose twitched, I was going with the latter.

Huck stopped at the entrance to Olive's yard, tail wagging and his bacon smile splashed across his face. "Sorry, buddy, we're heading to the beach." Just in case I changed my mind, he stayed an extra minute or two, short tail sort of just lobbing side to side now. By the time I reached the top of the series of wooden steps, he'd caught up and raced ahead of me down to the sand. Huck hadn't always been so enthusiastic about going down the hundreds of wooden steps. The first few times, I had to bring treats along and leave them on steps, a sort of bread crumb trail, to coax him down to the sand. Now, he flew over the stairs almost without touching them. He was just as fast on the way back up, whereas I was considerably slower.

I lived on an island where ocean surrounded me on all sides, but there was always something so exhilarating about stepping onto the sand and meeting face-to-face with the great Atlantic. It put all your senses on alert—seeing the frenzied activity of the various critters that called the coastline home, hearing the rhythmic sound of the waves rolling in and pulling out, smelling the tangy brine that wafted off the water, and, most of all, feeling the cool, salty sea breeze mingling with the warm sunshine.

Huck's main goal on a beach walk was to chase off any gulls or plovers that decided to trespass on his stretch of sand. For me, a walk on the shoreline was a chance to clear my head and marvel at nature. I walked straight to the water and stared out at the rippling ocean. Small waves curled their frothy heads, bowing to me as they rolled into shore. As the ocean pulled back, a number of treasures were uncovered, mostly stones rubbed smooth by the perpetual current. On this unveiling an unaware sand crab had suddenly found itself without its sandy cloak. It just as quickly burrowed back under it. I stooped down to pull free an Atlantic bay scallop and wasn't too surprised to discover that it was broken. With the current and rocks around the island, finding a shell whole and free of chips was rare.

Huck plopped down in the wet sand, satisfied that he'd scared off all the birds for good. I walked toward the dog, deciding to join him.

"Anna!" a voice called from the stairs.

I turned and held the brim of my straw hat to keep it from tumbling off my head. Seraphina and Samuel were about halfway down the endless flight of stairs. Sera was wearing a bright yellow sweat suit, so bright it almost hurt the eyes. Samuel, her handsome, young husband, reached the bottom first, then turned to offer a hand like a gentleman or footman might do for a woman exiting a carriage. Seraphina gave him her hand and a little kiss before hopping onto the sand.

I walked toward them, again holding my hat down and now wondering why I bothered with a straw hat on the beach. I'd pulled it off by the time I reached them. Sera was slightly out of breath, and her cheeks were red.

"Did you run here?" I asked.

"Just about." Sera smiled up at Samuel. "I did have a piggy back ride for part of the way."

"We came from the boarding house," Samuel said.

"Oh, I'm sorry. No one was in the mood for waffles, so I came down here for a walk."

Sera had finally caught her breath. "That's what Cora told us. She looked a little out of it." Sera pulled her lips in to hold back a smile. "Did she, you know—" Sera pretended to hold a bottle and tipped her head back to drink it.

"Was she drinking? No," I laughed. "However, she is suffering from a Junior Mint and brownie hangover."

Samuel laughed. "That explains the glassy, far off look in her eyes."

"The reason we stopped by the boarding house was because we overheard something at the 3Ts yesterday afternoon, something that might be important. An older couple, George and—"

"No, I think his name was John," Samuel said.

"I don't think so. Anyhow, it doesn't matter because they're long gone. They came to the island for the weekend to watch the pirate event, but since it ended early, they were traveling back to the mainland on the four o'clock ferry. At least, I think it was the four o'clock." She glanced up at Samuel. "Now you have me questioning everything."

Seraphina seemed to be taking the long route to the golden nugget. I just hoped it was worth the buildup.

"Just tell her the important part," Samuel prodded. I was giving him a high five with my mind.

"Right. So John or George—" she giggled. "Or maybe it was Paul or Ringo." She laughed again. "Anyhow, I can see a little bit of nostril flare on you, my friend, so I'll continue."

I had to resist the urge to pinch my nose because I envisioned unusually wide nostrils.

"George said that he and his wife—" She paused, rubbed her temple. "Never mind. I'm not going to even attempt a guess, but I do remember she drank hot tea with lemon and ate a cherry tart."

"You're doing this on purpose now," I said, dryly.

"Yes, I'm a stinker."

"They saw one of the role players with two guns," Samuel blurted.

Sera stared up at him with an arched brow. "Really?"

"Well, the day would be over before you spit it out, and I've got to fill the stockroom."

I waited for their rare moment of tension to end. Frankly, it was comforting to know that some existed in their otherwise fairy tale relationship.

"Anyhow," Sera went on, "George said at the time he just figured the man was supposed to have two guns, so he didn't think anything of it. Then he heard word that the person who killed Arvin had carried a real gun onto the battlefield. He wondered if that was why the guy had two guns."

"Did he get a look at the guy?"

"That's it. I guess between the costume and all the activity, he never saw the guy's face, but it was definitely one of the Spaniards."

"So it was a male?" I asked just to make sure.

"Yes."

Huck raced up from shore, soaking wet and looking like a sand monster.

He stopped and grinned up at all of us. We all ducked instinctively, knowing a twister of ocean and sand would follow. It was the longest, most productive shake any dog had ever pulled off. Even with our attempt to avoid the onslaught, we were all sufficiently coated.

"Some thank you, Huck, after I ran miles to find your mom and give her important information." Sera turned back to me. "Do you think it's important?

"Considering the scarce evidence I have to work with, it's a nice piece of information. If the man George saw was indeed hiding the real weapon in his costume, which is what I figured had happened, then I can narrow down the suspect list considerably. Thanks for running miles to find me." I winked at Samuel.

"You're welcome," Sera said.

"Well, babe, we need to head back to the 3Ts." Samuel wiped some of Huck's spray off his shirt. "I've got a lot of work to do."

"Yep, me too. You know what, Sammy, honey, go ahead and start back. I just want to talk to Anna for a second."

"Are you sure you're not going to need me behind you on the stairs?" Samuel asked.

I laughed. "Are you afraid she's going to fall?"

"No, he's not." Sera raised a second brow at him. "He just acts as a coach of sorts. Come on, Sera, you can do it. Keep those feet moving, that kind of thing."

"Otherwise, it could take her an hour to get to the top. She stops to rest… a lot."

Sera smiled sweetly up at him. "That's because I enjoy playing the damsel in distress." She lifted the back of her hand dramatically to her forehead. "Why, handsome prince, if I walk another step I may swoon."

"And you fall for that?" I asked Samuel.

"Not really but I pretend to."

Sera reached up and pinched his cheek. "My sweet prince. Now, run along, honey. I'll be right behind."

"No you won't," he called out as he headed toward the stairs.

Sera spun back around, her eyes glittering and a sly grin on her lips. "Guess who we saw when we went to find you at the house?"

"Cora? You already told me."

"Yes, yes, your bedraggled sister was sitting there in her robe."

"You say it as if she was sitting in the same tattered terry cloth robe I have hanging in my room. You might have noticed the gold Chanel logo on the pocket."

"I thought it looked familiar. Who buys a Chanel bathrobe? Never mind. I already know the answer to that. Anyhow, I was talking about a different tenant. He was pouring himself a cup of coffee."

"Ah, you met Nathaniel Smith. What did you think?"

"It was only the briefest of hellos after your sister begrudgingly introduced us. She hasn't sounded too enthusiastic about him, which surprised me because he might not be a billionaire but he's a looker. That's why I asked Samuel to go on without me. He gets so jealous when I talk about other men. How are you feeling about the new guy?"

"You mean do I think he's a looker? By the way, you might want to use a different phrase when you're talking about a handsome man because that one sort of dates you."

"I suppose but I hold onto those kinds of terms for when I want to talk to someone in my age group and I don't want Samuel to understand."

My laugh sent a seagull off. "I'm sorry. Is that like a parent spelling out the words *doctor* and *dentist* in front of their little ones so they don't know what's going on?"

"Sort of like that, I suppose." Sera and I walked toward the stairs together. Samuel had jogged all the way to the top. He stopped and waved down to us, then headed to the trail. "You haven't answered my question. And no, I'm not talking about his good looks. A woman would have to be dead and buried not to notice that man. He was just pouring coffee, and Cora and I held our breath watching him."

"Ah ha, no wonder Samuel seemed so contrary this morning. He usually agrees with everything you say."

Sera shrugged. "That's because I'm always right about everything."

We stopped at the bottom of the long chain of stairs and gazed up.

"Is this what climbers feel like when they stand at base camp and stare up at the Everest peak?" Sera asked.

I put my arm around her shoulder and gave her a squeeze. "I could walk behind you and toss out encouraging sentiments like 'you go girl'."

"You tried that in yoga class and it didn't work." Since we had no other choice, we began the climb to the top.

"Guess I wasn't a great cheerleader since you quit after the first class."

"That's because I fell over twice. It was the most humiliating hour of my life."

thirty-two

OPAL HAD BEEN ASKING about some of my homemade cinnamon rolls, and since I'd skipped the Sunday morning waffle extravaganza, I decided to bake a batch. Opal smelled the cinnamon and came down from her bedroom to help.

I handed her a bowl with a softened stick of butter. "One cup of brown sugar and a tablespoon of cinnamon, then whisk it together."

"Gotcha." Opal walked to the table with her ingredients and sat down. She was more of a sit down baker, but I appreciated the help and company.

I floured my soapstone counter and removed the yeast dough out of the proofing bowl. It was bubbly and light, the perfect consistency for flaky rolls.

"Anna, how is the investigation going?" Opal dumped the brown sugar into the bowl, then pulled a small chunk of it out of the container and pushed it between her lips.

"It's going... sort of. I actually received some information this morning that might help me narrow down the suspects. It's not anything definitive, which is where the 'sort of' came from." I pushed the rolling pin across the dough, floured it a little more and rolled it again.

"You'll catch 'em. You always do," Opal said confidently. "Did you know that Cary Grant's real name was Archibald Leach?" Opal never spent too much time on tedious topics like murder investigations when she could be talking about Hollywood.

"I think I knew Cary Grant was a stage name. It's such a nice, elegant name. It sounds like it was made up. But wow, Archibald Leach, that's a real clunker. Doesn't really fit the man at all, does it?" As I spoke, an inkling of an idea popped into my head, but it would have to wait until the cinnamon rolls were filled.

The door opened and some of the yeasty, cinnamon fragrance was replaced by the earthy, mossy smells wafting up from the river.

Tobias had decided on a bike ride after his morning swim. His cheeks were pink and his eyes sparkling from exertion. "Terrific morning for a bike ride." He walked straight to the sink to refill his flask with cold water. "I'm so glad to see the backside of that dreary, cold winter." He took a long drink, then lowered the flask. "Are my senses deceiving me or are there cinnamon rolls in the near future?"

"They do not deceive you." I noted. "They'll be ready after lunch."

Opal realized she had to stand up to give the butter and sugar a proper beating with the whisk.

Tobias returned to the sink to top off his flask again. "By the way, Anna," he spoke louder over the sound of the faucet, "the reenactment group is starting to pack up. They're all anxious to leave, and with an arrest made—they've been given permission to go."

"Argh," I grumbled and gave the rolling pin just a little too hard of a push. "Norwich has the wrong person. Now the true killer is going to casually climb onto the ferry and disappear into the abyss."

Tobias chuckled. "The city is crowded and, granted, it would be easier to hide there, but it's hardly an abyss."

"I know, Toby. You're right. It's just so frustrating to think that Norwich refuses to look past his nose on these investigations."

An unfamiliar sputtering motor rumbled outside the house.

"What on earth?" Tobias muttered. He walked to the front room window to look out. "Oh, it's *him*," he said with as much distaste as he could muster. "Looks like he bought a scooter. I'm heading upstairs to rest and catch up on some work." Tobias hurried off so quickly, I half expected to find burn marks in the floor.

Opal carried the bowl of filling over to the counter and smiled proudly as if she'd just created a culinary marvel. "I think these will be the best rolls ever. Now I think I'll head up for a little pre lunch nap." She took a deep whiff. "There will be visions of cinnamon rolls dancing in my head."

The kitchen door opened. "Cinnamon," Nathaniel said as

he entered. "Is there any other fragrance on earth that can conjure up as many memories as cinnamon?"

I paused my rolling pin to respond. "For a man who quotes, of all people, Tom Petty, that was a very thoughtful, sentimental comment."

"It's the cinnamon. Or maybe I'm feeling nostalgic because of my new set of wheels, a 2015 Trailmaster in race car red. When I was sixteen, I saved up all the money I earned working at my uncle's hardware store, then I bought myself a scooter that was more rust than paint. I spray painted it black and silver." He picked an apple out of the fruit bowl. "Boy, did I think I was something else on that thing, picking girls up for dates and everything. Except for the few dads who took one look at the thing and dragged their daughters back to the house." He took a bite of the apple. When he first stepped off of the ferry with his two bags and a sullen attitude that was deeper than the ocean floor, I worried the hard surface would never crack and we'd be stuck with a disagreeable housemate for six months. But the harsh façade was fading. It was the island. Frostfall Island brought out the best in people. Unless you had murder on your mind and that thought reminded me about the Cary Grant conversation. I needed to finish the cinnamon rolls and get back to the investigation before it was too late.

"Anna, do you have a tire pump?" Nathaniel asked. "I think the tires on my new wheels are a little flat. They were making a floppity-flop sound on the road."

"Yes, we have a pump in the garage."

"Great." He headed to the door. The shoulders were still

broad, but the tension had disappeared. He paused before stepping out. Huck was already at his heels to join him. That dog was probably the reason I knew the new guy would work out. Nathaniel's ocean blue gaze turned back to me. "And sorry about that quote, I guess I was feeling extra ornery that day."

"Probably because you caught your new landlord snooping around your personal belongings."

"Probably," he chuckled and walked out.

I returned to my task. I slathered the butter, brown sugar mixture across the dough, rolled it up and sliced it into a dozen rolls. Once I had them tucked into their buttered dish, I covered them for a second rise and washed my hands. My laptop was sitting on my desk with next week's grocery list still open on the screen. I typed Deke Silverton into the search bar and was instantly rewarded with his personal web page where he listed the various commercials and movie extra parts he'd done. Not exactly an illustrious career but then I wasn't there to find a lead actor. I was there to find a killer, and a bit of browsing handed me a big gold nugget. Deke Silverton was a stage name. His real name was Pete Dickson.

"That photo," I muttered. That was why the young boy looked familiar. I'd seen him before. That was why Arvin wanted to look at the list of names. He must have thought he recognized him. But how on earth was I going to prove Deke Silverton killed Arvin? It was going to take some thinking. In the meantime, I needed to get to North Pond before the camp was gone for good.

I rushed outside to the garage. I nearly ran right into Nathaniel as he stooped in the middle of the garage to fill the back tire on his scooter. His face snapped up when he heard me rush in. "Whoa, there landlady, where's the fire?"

"No fire but I've got to hurry to catch a killer. Just not sure how yet." I grabbed my bicycle.

"Ole Scooty McFlame can get you there quicker. Hop on. I promise to get you there in one piece. Wait. Where are we going exactly?"

I hesitated for a brief second, then parked my bike. "North Pond. But no jumps or wheelies."

Nathaniel laughed. "I don't think Scooty has a wheelie in him, but I'm not going to make promises about the jumps."

thirty-three

AFTER A FEW AWKWARD moments of trying to figure out where to place my hands, I finally rested them on Nathaniel's waist. His muscles tensed and relaxed beneath my hands. I was just as glad that he couldn't see the flustered pink flush on my face as we zipped along Island Drive.

I hadn't been on the back of a motorized vehicle for some time. I had to admit it was exhilarating and not just because of the broad shoulders in front of me. The wind in my face, the vast landscape flying by and the general rush one gets from moving quickly in fresh air helped energize me for the task ahead.

We reached the campsite. Tobias was exaggerating a bit, and I was thankful for that. While it seemed, in general, people were packing up belongings and personal campsites, the main tents for food and costumes were still standing.

Nathaniel looked back over his shoulder. "What does this killer look like? Or are we just going on a hunch."

"All my investigations are based on hunches. And that's worked out pretty well for me." I braced my hands on his shoulders as I climbed off the scooter. "I thank you for the ride, but I don't want to take up any more of your time." Since I had only a flimsy plan for catching the killer, I wasn't interested in being observed. Nathaniel had other plans.

He turned off the scooter. "No way. I want to see Anna St. James in action." He rubbed his hands together. "Where do we start? Or do we just yell 'hands on your head' and see who obeys?"

I stared at him with hands on hips. "If you're going to make light of this—"

He put up his hands. "Nope, sorry. I'll be a silent observer. You won't hear a peep out of me. Please proceed. I'll be your wingman. Besides, what if the killer makes a run for it? You're going to need Scooty to help chase 'em down."

I sighed. "Fine but no more sarcastic comments."

"Not one comment, sarcastic or otherwise." He followed along next to me, taking long strides to keep up with my harried pace. "Just here to watch the amazing St. James in action."

I stopped abruptly. He took a few steps past me then looked back. "Right. That probably fell into the sarcastic category, but I really am interested to see how you do this without any help from the professionals."

I scoffed. "Professionals, indeed. Only thing Norwich is expert at is chewing on a toothpick. But today, he's going to come in handy." We reached the center of the campsite. No one seemed to notice the visitors. I glanced around for my main suspect but didn't see him anywhere. I had a moment of despair as I considered that Deke had already left the island and that my whole plan had been obliterated, then he stepped out from the refreshment tent with a soda in his hand.

I whistled loud enough to get everyone's attention.

"Impressive," Nathanial muttered.

I gave him a side-eyed scowl.

"Right, no more comments." He drew an invisible zipper across his mouth.

"Everyone, I need your attention." Alan Jessup stepped out of his tent, shielding his eyes from the bright sunlight. I was going to need him for my plan. People gathered in somewhat reluctantly.

"I've just received a call from Detective Norwich. He is sending a team to do an evidence search of the costumes. He's looking specifically for gunfire residue in pockets."

I flicked my gaze toward Deke. He had stopped sipping his soda and was looking baffled and fidgety about the announcement. So were some of the others.

"But they've already arrested Barry Long," someone shouted. "Why are they looking at all the costumes? Barry was Captain Morgan."

"Apparently, Detective Norwich has decided to reopen the investigation." That bald-faced lie sent an irritated murmur around the crowd.

"He said we could pack up," someone said. "This isn't fair."

"That's why he's going to rush his team over here. Then

he can find the uniform with the residue and find out who was wearing the costume," I said.

"But wouldn't there be gun residue even from the prop guns? Even caps have a little gunpowder." This question came from Evie, the purported gun expert. She might very well have been right. I wasn't expecting her question, so I had to continue with my carnival of lies.

"Detective Norwich said they can tell whether live ammunition was fired according to the residue left behind. Like I said—they'll be quick about it. You can continue packing up. They'll be here soon."

I made a hasty retreat, not wanting to field any other questions from people who knew far more about guns than me. I headed toward the costume tent with my tagalong partner in tow.

"I think Norwich is pulling a fast one," Nathaniel said. "A forensics lab can probably detect some trace elements like lead or barium, something specific to a type of gun or bullet, but he'd have to take in all the costumes for analysis. Seems like a much bigger undertaking than you just relayed to everyone."

I shrugged. "Then it's a good thing Norwich isn't actually sending a team."

"Wait a minute. You made the whole thing up?"

I stopped and looked at him. "Yes and when we're done here, you can explain to me why you know so much about forensics."

He sealed his mouth shut and motioned with his hand for me to carry on.

I opened the flap on the costume tent. The racks were still filled with outfits, but the props had been boxed up and were ready to go. Jessup was pacing and rubbing his semi-bald head. He was chewing anxiously on his thumbnail.

"Mr. Jessup," I called, pulling him from his nervous pacing.

"I don't understand. Why didn't the detective let me know this was happening? I was just about to start packing up the costumes. This is going to cause a significant delay, and I was really hoping to get out on the last ferry of the evening."

"No problem," I said, calmly. "You'll still make it. I'm going to tell you a few things that I need you to keep to yourself."

"Is this about the murder? I knew Barry Long wasn't the killer. Sure, I'll do whatever it takes to get all this behind us."

"Thanks. I need you to leave the costume tent. Make a show of it. Talk to people, get some refreshments, let people see you so they know you've left the costumes alone."

"Ah, I see," Nathaniel muttered, then pulled his lips in to stop further comment.

Alan looked at Nathaniel warily. "Is this a police officer?"

I laughed. "Not exactly. But don't worry. I'll be here to keep an eye on the costumes. And remember, don't tell anyone that I asked you to leave the tent."

Alan nodded haltingly, then walked out.

"I don't think it was *that* funny," Nathaniel mumbled after the flap fell shut.

I glanced over at him, confused.

"When he asked if I was the police," he noted. "You

laughed as if it was the most ridiculous suggestion in the world."

"Come on, you have to admit, it was kind of funny." I didn't wait for him to agree. I grabbed his hand and pulled him along to the prop boxes piled in the corner. "We've got to hide. Our suspect could come in here any second."

We circled around the boxes and crouched down. I pushed a few boxes apart to make myself a peephole. Nathaniel did the same.

"This is the oddest stakeout I've ever seen," he commented but fell quickly silent when the flap on the tent opened. It shut just as quickly. When the harsh sun had stopped streaming into the tent, the tall silhouette came into view. Deke Silverton looked ashen gray with worry as he crept over to the rack of Spanish soldier costumes.

Deke flipped through the outfits, seemingly looking for the one he wore on reenactment day. He grew frustrated as he pushed aside each costume, then started again at the beginning. A clear bag hung over each piece making his task more difficult. He glanced back nervously toward the entrance, then turned back to the rack. He released a loud breath when he found the right costume. He pulled it free from the rack and looked anxiously around. It was time for me to act.

Nathaniel seemed surprised when I hopped to my feet and walked around the tower of boxes.

"Looking for a place to hide that?" I asked as I edged closer. I stopped at the end of the rack.

Deke stood there, eyes wide with surprise. He clutched the costume in his hands. "You shouldn't be in here," he said.

"Neither should you. But I guess you needed to hide the evidence before the police arrive." I stepped a little closer.

Fear flickered in his eyes as his gaze darted around the room looking for something, anything to get him out of his current predicament. "I have no idea what you're talking about." He licked his lips nervously. "I had no reason to kill Meeks. I hardly knew him."

"I don't know about that. If you grew up with someone, then you certainly knew him, *Pete*."

Hearing his real name made him flinch. He stared at me with that penetrating gaze, the one I saw in the old photo back from his carefree days, back when his brother was alive, back when he wasn't a murderer.

"Arvin destroyed my life." He was less agitated, and his tone was deep, dark. "Jumping the train was his idea. He always had stupid, dangerous schemes, and if we didn't go along with it, he'd tease us, call us chickens. Jimmy tried to talk all of us out of it, but Arvin mocked us, walked around clucking and flapping his arms like wings. Jimmy was going to go to medical school. He was the best big brother a guy could have," his voice broke. It was hard not to feel bad for the man, especially now that he'd destroyed his whole future. "My parents divorced. The whole family fell apart. Meeks deserved it. I'm not going to jail for something he deserved."

His whole sorrowful confession had caught me off guard. I didn't react quickly enough to get out of the way of the heavy rolling rack as it torpedoed toward me. It slammed into me. I fell backward so hard, it kicked the wind out of me. Pain shot up my back, and everything went black as I struggled to catch my breath.

thirty-four

AFTER A PANIC STRICKEN eternity struggling to breathe like a landed fish, I was finally able to suck in air. The shooting pain in my back had subsided to a dull ache. Colors and light returned along with the disappointing reality that my suspect had made a run for it.

I sat up and rubbed my tailbone, scanned the tent and was surprised to discover that my suspect had not made a clean getaway. I was even more surprised to find that my newest tenant had Deke facedown on the ground, his hands tied behind his back with a pirate sash. I might have still been seeing proverbial stars, but my hearing was not fuzzy. Nathaniel was reading Deke his rights. Most of us had heard those rights being read on television and in the movies, but Nathaniel was reciting them as if he'd done it many times... as a professional.

With a few grunts of pain, I pushed to my feet.

Nathaniel looked back over his shoulder. "How are you doing? Looked like the wind got knocked out of you."

"It sure did." I was walking a little slower than usual, but it seemed I'd escaped without any injuries, with the exception of a small bruise to my pride. I should have seen it coming. Deke's demeanor changed so quickly, it took me a second to process it, but there was no excuse for putting myself into such a vulnerable position. A rolling rack was an easy weapon, and it sure knocked me flat.

"Should probably call the police," Nathaniel said. "Unless you're in charge of making the actual arrest too."

I ignored his sarcasm and pulled out my phone. Mindy answered on one ring. "I'll bet you're going to tell me you've caught the real killer. They had to let Barry Long go this morning from lack of evidence. Norwich has been stomping around like a spoiled child throwing a tantrum because his toy broke."

"That's exactly what I'm envisioning. And yes, I have the real killer. Although I didn't catch him. I had help." I looked pointedly at my unofficial partner. He looked as cool as a cucumber as if he caught fleeing killers all the time. Something told me I wasn't far off on that assessment. "If Norwich can halt his tantrum long enough, maybe he could catch the next ferry back to the island and make an arrest."

"I'm going to get right on it." Mindy laughed lightly. "I can't wait to see his face turn red with rage when I tell him that Anna St. James bested him again. Thanks for making my day, friend."

"Anytime." I hung up. "Norwich should be here soon."

Deke had stopped struggling. He lay peacefully on the floor, his face to the side and his eyes closed as he seemingly contemplated his fate.

"It's a shame," I said quietly. "He kept so much anger all these years that it pushed him into a terrible decision."

Nathaniel looked down at him. "Hate will do that to a person. It eats you up inside until your soul is gone and your sense of reason goes with it." His words reminded me of his ominous comment when we met out on Chicory Trail. While the island seemed to be lightening his mood, it seemed there were still some demons hiding in his past, demons that had chased him all the way to Frostfall Island.

"That was impressive," Nathaniel said, dragging me from my thoughts.

"Yes, you certainly caught him easily, almost as if you've done this before," I added pointedly.

"I was talking about your scheme to catch him and corner him into a confession. You knew something about his past."

"His older brother died in a terrible tragedy, an accidental death brought on by a teenage stunt. Arvin Meeks, the victim, was the person who talked his brother into it. Deke's or, I should say, Pete's older brother died trying to keep him from getting hurt."

Deke sobbed without lifting his face from the floor. Again, my heart felt heavy for the man. It was a tragedy on top of a tragedy, and on top of that an innocent man lost his life. Arvin Meeks had made a bad decision in his youth. It came back to haunt him in adulthood.

Alan Jessup, who'd been reluctant to leave the costumes

and props, was worried enough to pop his head back inside and find out exactly what was going on. He spotted us standing over Deke and stepped inside, his eyes wide with shock.

"Deke," he said on a half gasp. "What's going on? I came in here to let you know there was no sign of the police yet but—" He stared down at Deke. The costume Deke had worn, the one he'd tried to hide from the evidence search was crumpled in its clear plastic bag on the floor just a few feet away.

"Mr. Jessup, Alan," I said calmly. "Please keep everyone out of this tent, and let us know the second Detective Norwich arrives. Mr. Smith and I will keep an eye on things here in the tent. Oh, and we don't need to let anyone know what's going on. Just tell them we received word from the detective that they are all free to pack up and go."

Jessup took one last, long look at the man on the ground. "Can't believe it." He shook his head and walked out of the tent.

"How long do you think it'll be?" Nathaniel asked.

"Depends on how anxious Norwich is to come and face me and admit, yet again, that he was wrong. Then there's the ferry schedule. Which reminds me." I pulled out my phone and texted Frannie. "We're going to need you to pick Norwich up from the mainland."

"That's fine. I'm leaving Bayberry Harbor right now."

"Great. Thanks."

"Did you solve another one?" she wrote back.

"Seems like I did."

"Woo hoo!"

I put my phone away. There was a question that had been dying to spring free, but I was waiting for the right time. It seemed as good a time as any, but before I could utter the words, Nathaniel turned his focus to Deke.

"Seems like we've got some time before the police get here. If you want to sit up, that's fine." Nathaniel glanced up at me. "I searched him and he's clean. Running would be a waste of time. As you might have noticed, we're on an island. Unless you're a really good swimmer, you won't get too far."

Deke moaned. It wasn't easy to sit up without the use of his hands but he managed. He stretched out his long legs and leaned against the nearby stack of boxes. He closed his eyes. Sadness pulled down the corners of his mouth.

Nathaniel and I stood near the flap, hoping to catch some of the fresh air slipping inside, all while keeping an ear out for the arrival of the police.

I had no more excuses. We were alone and there was nothing to do but wait. "Are you a cop?" I asked, bluntly. It seemed the easiest route to the truth.

He dropped his face and even shuffled his feet a little. He was like a kid trying to avoid having to spit out the truth.

"It's sort of obvious," I added, to let him know whatever excuse he came up with, it wasn't going to stick.

Nathaniel lifted his riveting blue gaze. For a second, I got lost in it. He took a deep breath. "I suppose if I tell you I watch a lot of cop shows on television—" I was shaking my head before he finished. "Right," he said. "I'm a cop. And I should probably just put all my cards on the table. Starting with this ace of spades—my name is not Nathaniel Smith. It's Nathaniel Maddon."

thirty-five

ALAN HAD several stools set up in front of a mirror at the far corner of the tent. We pulled them out and set them far enough away from our grim-faced suspect that he couldn't hear our conversation but close enough that we could grab him if he tried to run. From the look on his face, he had resolved to face the consequences of his actions. And those consequences would be serious indeed. Deke Silverton planned and successfully killed a man who, by all accounts, did nothing wrong. No prosecutor was going to allow sympathy for the assailant because the victim talked his brother into doing something dangerous back when they were teens.

"I imagine you have some questions," Nathaniel started, "but I'll just lay it all out and see if I've answered everything. First, a minor correction; I was a detective, but I'm no longer on the force. I turned my badge in three months ago. And, in case you were still worried—I am not the Pillow Talk Killer."

"No, uh, no I didn't think—"

"Yes you did," he said succinctly.

"Maybe for a second. In my defense, not many people keep a collection of articles about a serial killer. And—wait—why didn't you tell me you were a detective? I'm going on about how I do investigations on the island and my amateurish color-coded corkboards..." I placed my forehead on my palm. "So embarrassed. You must be thinking I'm the silliest woman alive." I looked up at him, but it wasn't easy.

"You're not even the tiniest bit silly. Can't say the same for some of the others in the house, but there is nothing silly about you, Anna St. James." He paused to look at me. For a fleeting moment, my breath was stolen again but in a different way. "To be honest, those color-coded corkboards are way more professional and organized than anything I had in my office. You did this whole investigation without any help from the police. I had a whole team of scientists, psychologists and experts at my disposal, but you did this over a cinnamon roll and coffee."

Some of my confidence had returned. I sat up a little straighter on the stool. "I did have some professional help today. He might have gotten away if you hadn't stepped in. It was such a stupid mistake."

"I agree with you there, only because you could have been hurt. People who have committed murder are rarely in their right minds. They also know if they've been caught they have nothing to lose. What you're doing is dangerous."

"I've been doing just fine, thank you," I said curtly.

Nathaniel stretched his legs out and crossed them at the

ankles. "All right. I won't go there. You're an adult, and it's not my business."

"Thank you but now I'm going to pry into your business. Why the fake name? Was the landlord's letter of reference fake too?"

"It was real. I'm sure Trevor just gave you the wrong phone number. He has the problem, you know, where the letters and numbers get mixed up on the page."

"Dyslexia?"

"That's it. I should have double-checked the number. The reason behind the fake name was I didn't want people to know where I was. That part about me wanting to get away from civilization? All true. After I turned in my badge, I wanted to get lost for awhile. I saw your advertisement for a boarding house room on Frostfall Island. I decided it was the perfect place to get away from the city."

"But why? Was it because of your ex-wife?"

"Nina? No. We hardly talk anymore. It was the job. It got to me. Every detective has one of those cases, a case that haunts their every waking hour, a case that just keeps getting away from them. For me—"

"The Pillow Talk Killer?" I asked.

"Yes."

A long pause followed as he stared down at the feet in front of him. "I couldn't let it happen again on my watch, so I took the cowardly way out and handed it off." He raked his fingers through his thick hair and lifted his gaze. "This monster, he charms his way into their lives, then murders them, brutally. He taunts the police with his sickly sweet messages. There would be times when I was sure we were closing in on him, then he'd disappear again, like he fell off the face of the earth. He did it on purpose. He would sense we were moving in and then he'd go quiet. But he never stayed in his hole or cave or whatever dark crevice he lived in between murders. All of it, all of it was just so frustrating." He groaned and rubbed his face with his hands. He lowered his arms. "So I slapped my badge down on the chief's desk and walked out. Never considered myself a quitter, but there's a first time for everything, apparently. There you have it. That's my humiliating, pathetic story."

"I don't think it's pathetic, and you're not a coward. I was reading about the PTK"—I looked pointedly at him—"yes, I was trying to find something that might connect you because I'm responsible for the people in my house and you were seemingly obsessed with the serial killer. I just never considered that your obsession was because you'd been trying to track him down. I'm sorry that I rushed to judgment."

"Well, I was being a huge heel about everything."

"Not going to argue there." I couldn't hold back a grin.

"Before you try and nudge in a little pep talk about how I'm not a coward and that I gave it the ole college try or whatever, there isn't anything you can say to make me feel better about myself."

"I agree." He looked somewhat surprised at my response. "Because the only person who can do that is you. I think you made the right choice coming to Frostfall Island. Yes, we have our share of mishaps—"

He chuckled. "Never heard murder described as a mishap but I like it."

"Aside from the mishaps, this island does something to a person. I don't know if it's the nature, that vast, endless ocean that on a clear day lets you see to the ends of the world or just because it's, as you say, away from civilization, but it's good for the soul. I know yours left you and hasn't returned, but I think, I hope, you'll find it again here on Frostfall Island."

His weak smile wasn't sad or lost, something I'd seen in his expression more than once. It was an 'I hope you're right' kind of smile.

The tent flap opened, shoving a streak of light through the space. It was Alan Jessup. "Detective Norwich just arrived." Before he could step inside, the tent flap wrenched back and Norwich burst in like a clumsy, arrogant, poorly dressed bull.

We stayed in our corner for a moment to observe without him knowing we were watching. He was like a great, eccentric movie character, an unlikable one, the guy who you disliked the second he walked on screen. He stared down at the suspect, sitting and leaning against the boxes with his hands secured behind his back. Deke stared up at him, trying to figure out just what was going on.

Norwich pulled the toothpick from his mouth long enough to bark at Jessup. "Where's St. James?"

Jessup's nervous gaze flicked toward the rear corner of the tent. Nathaniel and I stood up and headed toward the front. Norwich focused on me. His glare couldn't have been more clear. "St. James, what's this about? I don't even have this man on my list of suspects. There's a little thing called motive. You should look it up." He sneered as he jammed his toothpick back between his thin lips. Then, for the first time, he looked past me. His chin dropped and the toothpick fell to the ground. "Maddon, what are you doing here?"

My own chin did a bit of dropping as I spun back to look at Nathaniel. It explained his highly accurate description of Norwich.

"Not sure if that's any of your business, Norwich, but I see you're still the same old blustery fool you always were."

Norwich flared his nostrils, reached into his pocket and pulled out a replacement toothpick. "At least I'm not a quitter," he growled before sticking the toothpick between his lips.

"But the people in your jurisdiction would be a lot safer if you were."

Norwich gave him a narrowed eyed glare. The toothpick lifted up and down as he grinned. "How is that serial killer case going? Keeping all those young women safe?"

I sensed the heat coming off both men and had to pull the plug on the testosterone. "Can we please get to *this* case," I said.

Norwich pouted his lips out and managed to keep the toothpick locked in. "Aw, do you need to get home to bake some blueberry muffins?"

"If I did, why would that be such a bad thing?" I snapped. I was now at the end of the fishing line. "If you'd do your job correctly, then I wouldn't have to take time out of my day to catch the real killers. Mr. Silverton's name is actually Pete Dickson, and he has a tragic history with the victim. That's all I'm going to tell you except he confessed to killing Arvin Meeks. You can gather the rest of the case yourself. I'm through here. After all, those muffins aren't going to bake themselves." I flashed him a disdainful smile and walked out.

I paused outside, hoping Nathaniel would be right behind. The last thing anyone needed was the two men, who were obviously enemies, to start a fist fight. I released the breath I'd been holding when the flap opened and Nathaniel walked out, calmly, even smiling a bit.

"I forgot just how much I hated that guy," he muttered. "So, are you really making blueberry muffins because this whole adventure has worked up my appetite."

"Will cinnamon rolls do?"

"Definitely. I don't think it's just the island that'll help me find that part of me that left long ago. Your cooking might just be that magical boost I need to find myself." He patted his stomach. "And there'll be more of me to find too."

thirty-six

NATHANIEL HAD BEEN RIGHT. There was no other aroma like cinnamon to push you on a trip down memory lane. The kitchen swirled with the scent as we nibbled the cinnamon rolls. I'd added an extra layer of sugary glaze, possibly because I was happy to have solved the case but most likely because my baked goods always put a smile on everyone's face, even the new guy.

Nathaniel had taken his cinnamon roll upstairs. I'd hoped that he would stick around and chat, but I was still thrilled with the progress we'd made in our friendship. All the secrets, including the ones that had given me fitful sleep and a few stomachaches, had been cleared up and laid bare. I decided not to tell anyone else in the house about his former career. It wasn't my information to share.

Tobias stared down the table at Opal, who happily went on licking the sticky icing off her fingers. "There is such a thing as a napkin, Opal," he chided.

Opal peered at him through her purple framed glasses. "A napkin is used if you're eating pizza or a greasy burger, but sugary glaze should never be wasted. I just came up with that little household tip. Maybe I'll write a whole book of them," she mused.

Winston lifted his glass of milk. "I'd like to propose a toast to the brilliant woman who baked these cinnamon buns all while solving yet another murder. Here's to Anna!"

Glasses were raised. "Here's to Anna!" Everyone cheered.

"To Anna," a deep voice said from the doorway. Nathaniel was leaning against the doorjamb raising his empty milk glass.

I tried to subdue my smile and hold back a blush, but the latter was somewhat out of my control.

Cora winked at me, as if we had some big, bold sister secret going on between us but one of us, namely me, wasn't in on it. Then, suddenly, the secret exchange was gone, and she hopped up in her glittery pink dress.

"I just remembered something—Anna. I'd forgotten all about it. I brought the mail in yesterday. I know, everyone, it was my turn to sort it but I forgot. So I did it this morning—" she looked at everyone. "You're welcome," she said wryly. "There was a card for you, Anna. I think it's a birthday card. There was no return address—" She click-clacked away on her pink heels and came back with a blue envelope. "It's a little thicker than a card." She shook it next to her ear like a kid might shake one of the gifts under the Christmas tree.

"Are you expecting it to make a noise?" Winston asked with a laugh.

Cora shrugged. "I don't know. It just feels like there's something inside it." She handed me the envelope. My finger slid under the flap to pry it open. I realized the entire kitchen was holding a collective breath, in anticipation. Even Nathaniel had stuck around to witness the card opening.

I laughed. "Really? It's probably just a belated birthday card from my insurance agent or the phone company. Continue with your cinnamon roll feast and I'll reveal the mystery name in a second." I pulled out the card. The front was a watercolor of pink peonies. I opened the card. Something dropped out and fell in my lap. Before reading the card, I picked up the dried stem that had slipped out. I held it up in the light to get a better look at it.

Everyone's focus was back on me and my mysterious piece of mail. "What is that?" Tobias asked.

Before answering him, I glanced at the inside of the card. "Happy fortieth," was scrawled in sloppy writing. That was all they wrote. No signature. I stared at the dried flower in my fingers. "It's a dried purple larkspur."

Cora smiled. "Whoever sent that card knows what kind of flowers you like. You had pink peonies and purple larkspur in your wedding bouquet." My sister didn't remember that small detail out of sentimentality. To her, weddings were worthy of remembering in vivid detail, even small ones like mine.

"Well, don't keep us in suspense," Opal said. "Is it from one of your bridesmaids?"

It took me a second to process the question. "Cora was my only bridesmaid. The card isn't signed."

"That's strange," Winston said.

I looked at the larkspur one last time before pushing it back into the card. "I'm going to toss it. Like I said, it was probably just my insurance agent." I spoke airily, but the card had shaken me.

"Was your insurance agent at your wedding?" Nathaniel asked, even though he knew the answer.

"Nope," I said curtly to let him know the discussion about the card was over.

"It's probably from mom," Cora said. "She's getting kind of forgetful, so she probably didn't sign the card."

I nodded. "You're right. I'm sure that's who it's from. I'll call her later." I was under no illusion that my mom had remembered one detail about my small, insignificant wedding. It wasn't one of Cora's extravaganzas, after all. I could have carried a bouquet of live snakes down the aisle, and my mom wouldn't have remembered.

"Now where were we?" I picked up my glass of milk. "There was something about the brilliant baker of these cinnamon rolls." I lifted the glass and everyone cheered again. I put the glass to my lips and took a sip, as I did my gaze drifted to the man in the doorway. He gave me a knowing look. He knew the card had upset me. I pulled my gaze away from his, but it wasn't easy.

I pushed the card aside, determined not to let it ruin a wonderful day. After all, I was sitting in my favorite kitchen, with my favorite band of merry misfits, enjoying some freshly baked cinnamon rolls and, to top it all off, I'd solved yet another Frostfall Island murder.

Death by Rocky Road - Book 2

about the author

London Lovett is author of the Port Danby, Starfire, Firefly Junction and Frostfall Island Cozy Mystery series. She loves getting caught up in a good mystery and baking delicious, new treats!

Learn more at:
www.londonlovett.com

Printed in Great Britain
by Amazon